George Sylvester Viereck

The House
of the Vampire

UltraLetters Publishing

Title: The House of the Vampire

Author: George Sylvester Viereck

First Edition: 1907

Cover: Underwood & Underwood

ISBN : 978-2-930718-17-0

www.UltraLetters.com

UltraLetters Publishing, Brussels.
contact@UltraLetters.com

Contents

Chapter 1

The freakish little leader of the orchestra, newly imported from Sicily to New York, tossed his conductor's wand excitedly through the air, drowning with musical thunders the hum of conversation and the clatter of plates.

Yet neither his apish demeanour nor the deafening noises that responded to every movement of his agile body detracted attention from the figure of Reginald Clarke and the young man at his side as they smilingly wound their way to the exit.

The boy's expression was pleasant, with an inkling of wistfulness, while the soft glimmer of his lucid eyes betrayed the poet and the dreamer. The smile of Reginald Clarke was the smile of a conqueror. A suspicion of silver in his crown of dark hair only added dignity to his bearing, while the infinitely ramified lines above the heavy-set mouth spoke at once of subtlety and of strength. Without stretch of the imagination one might have likened him to a Roman cardinal of the days of the Borgias, who had miraculously stepped forth from the time-stained canvas and slipped into twentieth century evening-clothes.

With the affability of complete self-possession he nodded in response to greetings from all sides, inclining his head with special politeness to a young woman whose sea-blue eyes were riveted upon his features with a look of mingled hate and admiration.

The woman, disregarding his silent salutation, continued to stare at him wild-eyed, as a damned soul in purgatory might look at Satan passing in regal splendour through the seventy times sevenfold circles of hell.

Reginald Clarke walked on unconcernedly through the rows of gay diners, still smiling, affable, calm. But his companion bethought himself of certain rumours he had heard concerning Ethel

Brandenbourg's mad love for the man from whose features she could not even now turn her eyes. Evidently her passion was unreciprocated. It had not always been so. There was a time in her career, some years ago in Paris, when it was whispered that she had secretly married him and, not much later, obtained a divorce. The matter was never cleared up, as both preserved an uncompromising silence upon the subject of their matrimonial experience. Certain it was that, for a space, the genius of Reginald Clarke had completely dominated her brush, and that, ever since he had thrown her aside, her pictures were but plagiarisms of her former artistic self.

The cause of the rupture between them was a matter only of surmise; but the effect it had on the woman testified clearly to the remarkable power of Reginald Clarke. He had entered her life and, behold! the world was transfixed on her canvases in myriad hues of transcending radiance; he had passed from it, and with him vanished the brilliancy of her colouring, as at sunset the borrowed amber and gold fade from the face of the clouds.

The glamour of Clarke's name may have partly explained the secret of his charm, but, even in circles where literary fame is no pass-port, he could, if he chose, exercise an almost terrible fascination. Subtle and profound, he had ransacked the coffers of medieval dialecticians and plundered the arsenals of the Sophists. Many years later, when the vultures of misfortune had swooped down upon him, and his name was no longer mentioned without a sneer, he was still remembered in New York drawing-rooms as the man who had brought to perfection the art of talking. Even to dine with him was a liberal education.

Clarke's marvellous conversational power was equalled only by his marvellous style. Ernest Fielding's heart leaped in him at the thought that henceforth he would be privileged to live under one roof with the only writer of his generation who could lend to the English language the rich strength and rugged music of the Elizabethans.

Reginald Clarke was a master of many instruments. Milton's mighty organ was no less obedient to his touch than the little lute of the troubadour. He was never the same; that was his strength. Clarke's style possessed at once the chiselled chasteness of a Greek marble column and the elaborate deviltry of the late Renaissance. At times his winged words seemed to flutter down the page frantically like Baroque angels; at other times nothing could have more adequately described his manner than the timeless calm of the gaunt pyramids.

The two men had reached the street. Reginald wrapped his long spring coat round him. "I shall expect you to-morrow at four," he said.

The tone of his voice was deep and melodious, suggesting hidden depths and cadences. "I shall be punctual."

The younger man's voice trembled as he spoke.

"I look forward to your coming with much pleasure. I am interested in you." The glad blood mounted to Ernest's cheeks at praise from the austere lips of this arbiter of literary elegance.

An almost imperceptible smile crept over the other man's features.

"I am proud that my work interests you," was all the boy could say.

"I think it is quite amazing, but at present," here Clarke drew out a watch set with jewels, "I am afraid I must bid you good-bye."

He held Ernest's hand for a moment in a firm genial grasp, then turned away briskly, while the boy remained standing open-mouthed. The crowd jostling against him carried him almost off his feet, but his eyes followed far into the night the masterful figure of Reginald Clarke, toward whom he felt himself drawn with every fiber of his body and the warm enthusiasm of his generous youth.

Chapter 2

With elastic step, inhaling the night-air with voluptuous delight, Reginald Clarke made his way down Broadway, lying stretched out before him, bathed in light and pulsating with life.

His world-embracing intellect was powerfully attracted by the Giant City's motley activities. On the street, as in the salon, his magnetic power compelled recognition, and he stepped through the midst of the crowd as a Circassian blade cleaves water.

After walking a block or two, he suddenly halted before a jeweller's shop. Arrayed in the window were priceless gems that shone in the glare of electricity, like mystical serpent-eyes—— green, pomegranate and water-blue. And as he stood there the dazzling radiance before him was transformed in the prism of his mind into something great and very wonderful that might, some day, be a poem.

Then his attention was diverted by a small group of tiny girls dancing on the sidewalk to the husky strains of an old hurdy-gurdy. He joined the circle of amused spectators, to watch those pink-ribboned bits of femininity swaying airily to and fro in unison with the tune. One especially attracted his notice—a slim olive-coloured girl from a land where it is always spring. Her whole being translated into music, with hair dishevelled and feet hardly touching the ground, the girl suggested an orange-leaf dancing on a sunbeam. The rasping street-organ, perchance, brought to her melodious reminiscences of some flute-playing Savoyard boy, brown-limbed and dark of hair.

For several minutes Reginald Clarke followed with keen delight each delicate curve her graceful limbs described. Then—was it that she grew tired, or that the stranger's persistent scrutiny embarrassed her?—the music oozed out of her movements. They grew slower, angular, almost clumsy. The look of interest in Clarke's eyes died, but his whole form quivered, as if the rhythm of the music and the dance had mysteriously entered into his blood.

He continued his stroll, seemingly without aim; in reality he followed, with nervous intensity, the multiform undulations of the populace, swarming through Broadway in either direction. Like the giant whose strength was rekindled every time he touched his mother, the earth, Reginald Clarke seemed to draw fresh vitality from every contact with life.

He turned east along Fourteenth street, where cheap vaudevilles are strung together as glass- pearls on the throat of a wanton. Gaudy bill-boards, drenched in clamorous red, proclaimed the tawdry attractions within. Much to the surprise of the doorkeeper at a particularly evil-looking music hall, Reginald Clarke lingered in the lobby, and finally even bought a ticket that entitled him to enter this sordid wilderness of décolleté art. Street-snipes, a few workingmen, dilapidated sportsmen, and women whose ruined youth thick layers of powder and paint, even in this artificial light, could not restore, constituted the bulk of the audience. Reginald Clarke, apparently unconscious of the curiosity, surprise and envy that his appearance excited, seated himself at a table near the stage, ordering from the solicitous waiter only a cocktail and a programme. The drink he left untouched, while his eyes greedily ran down the lines of the announcement. When he had found what he sought, he lit a cigar, paying no attention to the boards, but studying the audience with cursory interest until the appearance of Betsy, the Hyacinth Girl.

When she began to sing, his mind still wandered. The words of her song were crude, but not without a certain lilt that delighted the uncultured ear, while the girl's voice was thin to the point of being unpleasant. When, however, she came to the burden of the song, Clarke's manner changed suddenly. Laying down his cigar, he listened with rapt attention, eagerly gazing at her. For, as she sang the last line and tore the hyacinth-blossoms from her hair, there crept into her voice a strangely poignant, pathetic little thrill, that redeemed the execrable faultiness of her singing, and brought the rude audience under her spell.

Clarke, too, was captivated by that tremour, the infinite sadness of which suggested the plaint of souls moaning low at night, when lust preys on creatures marked for its spoil.

The singer paused. Still those luminous eyes were upon her. She grew nervous. It was only with tremendous difficulty that she reached the refrain. As she sang the opening lines of the last stanza, an inscrutable smile curled on Clarke's lips. She noticed the man's relentless gaze and faltered. When the burden came, her singing was hard and cracked: the tremour had gone from her voice.

Chapter 3

Long before the appointed time Ernest walked up and down in front of the abode of Reginald Clarke, a stately apartment-house overlooking Riverside Drive.

Misshapen automobiles were chasing by, carrying to the cool river's marge the restlessness and the fever of American life. But the bustle and the noise seemed to the boy only auspicious omens of the future.

Jack, his room-mate and dearest friend, had left him a month ago, and, for a space, he had felt very lonely. His young and delicate soul found it difficult to grapple with the vague fears that his nervous brain engendered, when whispered sounds seemed to float from hidden corners, and the stairs creaked under mysterious feet.

He needed the voice of loving kindness to call him back from the valley of haunting shadows, where his poet's soul was wont to linger overlong; in his hours of weakness the light caress of a comrade renewed his strength and rekindled in his hand the flaming sword of song.

And at nightfall he would bring the day's harvest to Clarke, as a worshipper scattering precious stones, incense and tapestries at the feet of a god.

Surely he would be very happy. And as the heart, at times, leads the feet to the goal of its desire, while multicoloured dreams, like dancing-girls, lull the will to sleep, he suddenly found himself stepping from the elevator-car to Reginald Clarke's apartment.

Already was he raising his hand to strike the electric bell when a sound from within made him pause half-way.

"No, there's no help!" he heard Clarke say. His voice had a hard, metallic clangour. A boyish voice answered plaintively. What the words were Ernest could not distinctly hear, but the suppressed sob in them almost brought the tears to his eyes. He instinctively knew that this was the finale of some tragedy.

He withdrew hastily, so as not to be a witness of an interview that was not meant for his ears. Reginald Clarke probably had good reason for parting with his young friend, whom Ernest surmised to be Abel Felton, a talented boy, whom the master had taken under his wings.

In the apartment a momentary silence had ensued. This was interrupted by Clarke: "It will come again, in a month, in a year, in two years."

"No, no! It is all gone!" sobbed the boy.

"Nonsense. You are merely nervous. But that is just why we must part. There is no room in one house for two nervous people."

"I was not such a nervous wreck before I met you. "Am I to blame for it—for your morbid fancies, your extravagance, the slow tread of a nervous disease, perhaps?"

"Who can tell? But I am all confused. I don't know what I am saying. Everything is so puzzling—life, friendship, you. I fancied you cared for my career, and now you end our friendship without a thought!"

"We must all follow the law of our being."

"The laws are within us and in our control."

"They are within us and beyond us. It is the physiological structure of our brains, our nerve- cells, that makes and mars our lives.

"Our mental companionship was so beautiful. It was meant to last."

"That is the dream of youth. Nothing lasts. Everything flows—panta rei. We are all but sojourners in an inn. Friendship, as love, is an illusion. Life has nothing to take from a man who has no illusions."

"It has nothing to give him."

They said good-bye.

At the door Ernest met Abel.

"Where are you going?" he asked. "For a little pleasure trip."

Ernest knew that the boy lied.

He remembered that Abel Felton was at work upon some book, a play or a novel. It occurred to him to inquire how far he had progressed with it.

Abel smiled sadly. "I am not writing it."

"Not writing it?"

"Reginald is."

"I am afraid I don't understand."

"Never mind. Some day you will."

Chapter 4

"I am so happy you came," Reginald Clarke said, as he conducted Ernest into his studio. It was a large, luxuriously furnished room overlooking the Hudson and Riverside Drive.

Dazzled and bewildered, the boy's eyes wandered from object to object, from picture to statue. Despite seemingly incongruous details, the whole arrangement possessed style and distinction.

A satyr on the mantelpiece whispered obscene secrets into the ears of Saint Cecilia. The argent limbs of Antinous brushed against the garments of Mona Lisa. And from a corner a little rococo lady peered coquettishly at the gray image of an Egyptian sphinx. There was a picture of Napoleon facing the image of the Crucified. Above all, in the semidarkness, artificially produced by heavy draperies, towered two busts.

"Shakespeare and Balzac!" Ernest exclaimed with some surprise. "Yes," explained Reginald, "they are my gods."

His gods! Surely there was a key to Clarke's character. Our gods are ourselves raised to the highest power.

Clarke and Shakespeare!

Even to Ernest's admiring mind it seemed almost blasphemous to name a contemporary, however esteemed, in one breath with the mighty master of song, whose great gaunt shadow, thrown against the background of the years has assumed immense, unproportionate, monstrous dimensions.

Yet something might be said for the comparison. Clarke undoubtedly was universally broad, and undoubtedly concealed, with no less exquisite taste than the Elizabethan, his own personality under the splendid raiment of his art. They certainly were affinities. It would not have been surprising to him to see the clear calm head of Shakespeare rise from behind his host.

Perhaps—who knows?—the very presence of the bust in his room had, to some extent, subtly and secretly moulded Reginald Clarke's life. A man's soul, like the chameleon, takes colour from its environment. Even comparative trifles, the number of the house in which we live, or the colour of the wallpaper of a room, may determine a destiny.

The boy's eyes were again surveying the fantastic surroundings in which he found himself; while, from a corner, Clarke's eyes were watching his every movement, as if to follow his thoughts into the innermost labyrinth of the mind. It seemed to Ernest, under the spell of this passing fancy, as though each vase, each picture, each curio in the room, was reflected in Clarke's work. In a long-queued, porcelain Chinese mandarin he distinctly recognised a quaint quatrain in one of Clarke's most marvellous poems. And he could have sworn that the grin of the

Hindu monkey-god on the writing-table reappeared in the weird rhythm of two stanzas whose grotesque cadence had haunted him for years.

At last Clarke broke the silence. "You like my studio?" he asked. The simple question brought Ernest back to reality.

"Like it? Why, it's stunning. It set up in me the queerest train of thought."

"I, too, have been in a whimsical mood tonight. Fancy, unlike genius, is an infectious disease."

"What is the peculiar form it assumed in your case?"

"I have been wondering whether all the things that environ us day by day are, in a measure, fashioning our thought-life. I sometimes think that even my little mandarin and this monkey-idol which, by the way, I brought from India, are exerting a mysterious but none the Less real influence upon my work."

"Great God!" Ernest replied, "I have had the identical thought!"

"How very strange!" Clarke exclaimed, with seeming surprise.

"It is said tritely but truly, that great minds travel the same roads," Ernest observed, inwardly pleased.

"No," the older man subtly remarked, "but they reach the same conclusion by a different route."

"And you attach serious importance to our fancy?"

"Why not?"

Clarke was gazing abstractedly at the bust of Balzac. "A man's genius is commensurate with his ability of absorbing from life the elements essential to his artistic completion. Balzac possessed this power in a remarkable degree. But, strange to say, it was evil that attracted him most. He absorbed it as a sponge absorbs water; perhaps because there was so little of it in his own make-up. He must have purified the atmosphere around him for miles, by bringing all the evil that was floating in the air or slumbering in men's souls to the point of his pen.

"And he"—his eyes were resting on Shakespeare's features as a man might look upon the face of a brother—"he, too, was such a nature. In fact, he was the most perfect type of the artist. Nothing escaped his mind. From life and from books he drew his material, each time reshaping it with a master-hand. Creation is a divine prerogative. Re-creation, infinitely more wonderful than mere calling into existence, is the prerogative of the poet. Shakespeare took his colours from many palettes. That is why he is so great, and why his work is incredibly greater than be. It alone explains his unique achievement. Who was he? What education did he have, what opportunities? None. And yet we find in his work the wisdom of Bacon, Sir Walter Raleigh's fancies and discoveries, Marlowe's verbal thunders and the mysterious loveliness of Mr. W. H."

Ernest listened, entranced by the sound of Clarke's melliflous voice. He was, indeed, a master of the spoken word, and possessed a miraculous power of giving to the wildest fancies an air of vraisemblance.

Chapter 5

"Yes," said Walkham, the sculptor, "it's a most curious thing."

"What is?" asked Ernest, who had been dreaming over the Sphinx that was looking at him from its corner with the sarcastic smile of five thousand years.

"How our dreams of yesterday stare at us like strangers to-day."

"On the contrary," remarked Reginald, "it would be strange if they were still to know us. In fact, it would be unnatural. The skies above us and the earth underfoot are in perpetual motion. Each atom of our physical nature is vibrating with unimaginable rapidity. Change is identical with life."

"It sometimes seems," said the sculptor, "as if thoughts evaporated like water."

"Why not, under favorable conditions?"

"But where do they go? Surely they cannot perish utterly?"

"Yes, that is the question. Or, rather, it is not a question. Nothing is ever lost in the spiritual universe."

"But what," inquired Ernest, "is the particular reason for your reflection?"

"It is this," the sculptor replied; "I had a striking motive and lost it."

"Do you remember," he continued, speaking to Reginald, "the Narcissus I was working on the last time when you called at my studio?"

"Yes; it was a striking thing and impressed me very much, though I cannot recall it at the moment."

"Well, it was a commission. An eccentric young millionaire had offered me eight thousand dollars for it. I had an absolutely original conception. But I cannot execute it. It's as if a breeze had carried it away."

"That is very regrettable."

"'Well, I should say so," replied the sculptor. Ernest smiled. For everybody knew of Walkham's domestic troubles. Having twice figured in the divorce court, he was at present defraying the expenses of three households.

The sculptor had meanwhile seated himself at Reginald's writing-table, unintentionally scanning a typewritten page that was lying before him. Like all artists, something of a madman and something of a child, he at first glanced over its contents distractedly, then with an interest so intense that he was no longer aware of the impropriety of his action.

"By Jove!" he cried. "What is this?"

"It's an epic of the French Revolution," Reginald replied, not without surprise.

"But, man, do you know that I have discovered my motive in it?"

"What do you mean?" asked Ernest, looking first at Reginald and then at Walkham, whose sanity he began to doubt.

"Listen!"

And the sculptor read, trembling with emotion, a long passage whose measured cadence delighted Ernest's ear, without, however, enlightening his mind as to the purport of Walkham's cryptic remark.

Reginald said nothing, but the gleam in his eye showed that this time, at least, his interest was alert.

Walkham saw the hopelessness of making clear his meaning without an explanation.

"I forget you haven't a sculptor's mind. I am so constituted that, with me, all impressions are immediately translated into the sense of form. I do not hear music; I see it rise with domes and spires, with painted windows and Arabesques. The scent of the rose is to me tangible. I can almost feel it with my hand. So your prose suggested to me, by its rhythmic flow, something which, at first indefinite, crystallised finally into my lost conception of Narcissus."

"It is extraordinary," murmured Reginald. "I had not dreamed of it."

"So you do not think it rather fantastic?" remarked Ernest, circumscribing his true meaning.

"No, it is quite possible. Perhaps his Narcissus was engaging the subconscious strata of my mind while I was writing this passage. And surely it would be strange if the undercurrents of our mind were not reflected in our style."

"Do you mean, then, that a subtle psychologist ought to be able to read beneath and between our lines, not only what we express, but also what we leave unexpressed?"

"Undoubtedly."

"Even if, while we are writing, we are unconscious of our state of mind? That would open a new field to psychology."

"Only to those that have the key, that can read the hidden symbols. It is to me a matter-of- course that every mind-movement below or above the threshold of consciousness must, of a necessity, leave its imprint faintly or clearly, as the case may be, upon our activities.

"This may explain why books that seem intolerably dull to the majority, delight the hearts of the few," Ernest interjected.

"Yes, to the few that possess the key. I distinctly remember how an uncle of mine once laid down a discussion on higher mathematics and blushed fearfully when his innocent wife looked over his shoulder. The man who had written it was a roué."

"Then the seemingly most harmless books may secretly possess the power of scattering in young minds the seed of corruption," Walkham remarked.

"If they happen to understand," Clarke observed thoughtfully. "I can very well conceive of a lecherous text-book of the calculus, or of a reporter's story of a picnic in which burnt, under the surface, undiscoverable, save to the initiate, the tragic passion of Tristram and Iseult."

Chapter 6

Several weeks had elapsed since the conversation in Reginald Clarke's studio. The spring was now well advanced and had sprinkled the meadows with flowers, and the bookshelves of the reviewers with fiction. The latter Ernest turned to good account, but from the flowers no poem blossomed forth. In writing about other men's books, he almost forgot that the springtide had brought to him no bouquet of song. Only now and then, like a rippling of water, disquietude troubled his soul.

The strange personality of the master of the house had enveloped the lad's thoughts with an impenetrable maze. The day before Jack had come on a flying visit from Harvard, but even he was unable to free Ernest's soul from the obsession of Reginald Clarke.

Ernest was lazily stretching himself on a couch, waving the smoke of his cigarette to Reginald, who was writing at his desk.

"Your friend Jack is delightful," Reginald remarked, looking up from his papers. "And his ebon-coloured hair contrasts prettily with the gold in yours. I should imagine that you are temperamental antipodes."

"So we are; but friendship bridges the chasm between."

"How long have you known him?"

"We have been chums ever since our sophomore year."

"What attracted you in him?"

"It is no simple matter to define exactly one's likes and dislikes. Even a tiny protoplasmic animal appears to be highly complex under the microscope. How can we hope to analyse, with any degree of certitude, our souls, especially when, under the influence of feeling, we see as through a glass darkly."

"It is true that personal feeling colours our spectacles and distorts the perspective. Still, we should not shrink from self-analysis. We must learn to see clearly into our own hearts if we would give vitality to our work. Indiscretion is the better part of literature, and it behooves us to hound down each delicate elusive shadow of emotion, and convert it into copy."

"It is because I am so self-analytical that I realise the complexity of my nature, and am at a loss to define my emotions. Conflicting forces sway us hither and thither without neutralising each other. Physicology isn't physics. There were many things to attract me to jack. He was subtler, more sympathetic, more feminine, perhaps, than the rest of my college-mates."

"That I have noticed. In fact, his lashes are those of a girl. You still care for him very much?"

"It isn't a matter of caring. We are two beings that live one life."

"A sort of psychic Siamese twins?"

"Almost. Why, the matter is very simple. Our hearts root in the same soil; the same books have nourished us, the same great winds have shaken our being, and the same sunshine called forth the beautiful blossom of friendship."

"He struck me, if you will pardon my saying so, as a rather commonplace companion."

"There is in him a hidden sweetness, and a depth of feeling which only intimate contact reveals. He is now taking his post-graduate course at Harvard, and for well-nigh two months we have not met; yet so many invisible threads of common experience unite us that we could meet after years and still be near each other."

"You are very young," Reginald replied. "What do you mean?"

"Ah—never mind."

"So you do not believe that two hearts may ever beat as one?"

"No, that is an auditory delusion. Not even two clocks beat in unison. There is always a discrepancy, infinitesimal, perhaps, but a discrepancy nevertheless."

A sharp ring of the bell interrupted the conversation. A moment later a curly head peeped through the door.

"Hello, Ernest! How are you, old man the intruder cried, with a laugh in his voice. Then, noticing Clarke, he shook hands with the great man unceremoniously, with the nonchalance of the healthy young animal bred in the atmosphere of an American college.

His touch seemed to thrill Clarke, who breathed heavily and then stepped to the window, as if to conceal the flush of vitality on his cheek.

It was a breath of springtide that Jack had brought with him. Youth is a Prince Charming. To shrivelled veins the pressure of his hand imparts a spark of animation, and middle age unfolds its petals in his presence, as a sunflower gazing at late noon once more upon its lord.

"I have come to take Ernest away from you," said Jack. "He looks a trifle paler than usual, and a day's outing will stir the red corpuscles in his blood."

"I have no doubt that you will take very good care of him," Reginald replied.

"Where shall we go?" Ernest asked, absent-mindedly.

But he did not hear the answer, for Reginald's scepticisms had more deeply impressed him than he cared to confess to himself.

Chapter 7

The two boys had bathed their souls in the sea-breeze, and their eyes in light.

The tide of pleasure-loving humanity jostling against them had carried their feet to the "Lion Palace." From there, seated at table and quenching their thirst with high-balls, they watched the feverish palpitations of the city's life-blood pulsating in the veins of Coney Island, to which they had drifted from Brighton Beach.

Ernest blew thoughtful rings of smoke into the air.

"Do you notice the ferocious look in the mien of the average frequenter of this island resort?" he said to Jack, whose eyes, following the impulse of his more robust youth, were examining specimens of feminine flotsam on the waves of the crowd.

"It is," he continued, speaking to himself for want of an audience, "the American who is in for having a 'good time.' And he is going to get it. Like a huntsman, he follows the scent of happiness; but I warrant that always it eludes him. Perhaps his mad race is only the epitome of humanity's vain pursuit of pleasure, the eternal cry that is never answered."

But Jack was not listening. There are times in the life of every man when a petticoat is more attractive to him than all the philosophy of the world.

Ernest was a little hurt, and it was not without some silent remonstrance that he acquiesced when jack invited to their table two creatures that once were women.

"Why?"

"But they are interesting."

"I cannot find so."

They both had seen better times—of course. Then money losses came, with work in shop or factory, and the voice of the tempter in the commercial wilderness.

One, a frail nervous little creature, who had instinctively chosen a seat at Ernest's side, kept prattling in his ear, ready to tell the story of her life to any one who was willing to treat her to a drink. Something in her demeanour interested him.

"And then I had a stroke of luck. The manager of a vaudeville was my friend and decided to give me a trial. He thought I had a voice. They called me Betsy, the Hyacinth Girl. At first it seemed as if people liked to hear me. But I suppose that was because I was new. After a month or two they discharged."

"And why?"

"I suppose I was just used up, that's all."

"Frightful!"

"I never had much of a voice—and the tobacco smoke—and the wine—I love wine." She gulped down her glass.

"And do you like your present occupation?"

"Why not? Am I not young? Am I not pretty?"

This she said not parrotwise, but with a simple coquettishness that was all her own. On the way to the steamer a few moments later, Ernest asked, half-reproachfully: "Jack—and you really enjoyed this conversation?"

"Didn't you?"

"Do you mean this?"

"Why, yes; she was—very agreeable." Ernest frowned.

"We're twenty, Ernest. And then, you see, it's like a course in sociology. Susie—"

"Susie, was that her name?"

"Yes."

"So she had a name?"

"Of course."

"She shouldn't. It should be a number."

"They may not be pillars of society; still, they're human."

"Yes," said Ernest, "that is the most horrible part of it."

Chapter 8

The moon was shining brightly.

Swift and sure the prow of the night-boat parted the silvery foam. The smell of young flesh. Peals of laughter. A breathless pianola. The tripping of dancing-feet. Voices husked with drink and voices soft with love. The shrill accents of vulgarity. Hustling waiters. Shop-girls. Bourgeois couples. Tired families of four and upward. Sleeping children. A boy selling candy. The crying of babies.

The two friends were sitting on the upper deck, muffled in their long rain-coats. In the distance the Empire City rose radiant from the mist.

"Say, Ernest, you should spout some poetry as of old. Are your lips stricken mute, or are you still thinking of Coney Island?"

"Oh, no, the swift wind has taken it away. I am clean, I am pure. Life has passed me. It has kissed me, but it has left no trace."

He looked upon the face of his friend. Their hands met. They felt, with keen enjoyment, the beauty of the night, of their friendship, and of the city beyond.

Then Ernest's lips moved softly, musically, twitching with a strange ascetic passion that trembled in his voice as he began:

"Huge steel-ribbed monsters rise into the air

Her Babylonian towers, while on high,

Like gilt-scaled serpents, glide the swift trains by,

Or, underfoot, creep to their secret lair.

A thousand lights are jewels in her hair,

The sea her girdle, and her crown the sky;

Her life-blood throbs, the fevered pulses fly.

Immense, defiant, breathless she stands there.

"And ever listens in the ceaseless din,

Waiting for him, her lover, who shall come,

Whose singing lips shall boldly claim their own,

And render sonant what in her was dumb,

The splendour, and the madness, and the sin,

Her dreams in iron and her thoughts of stone."

He paused. The boat glided on. For a long time neither spoke a word. After a while Jack broke the silence: "And are you dreaming of becoming the lyric mouth of the city, of giving utterance to all its yearnings, its 'dreams in iron and its thoughts of stone'?"

"No," replied Ernest, simply, "not yet. It is strange to what impressions the brain will respond. In Clarke's house, in the midst of inspiring things, inspiration failed me. But while I was with that girl an idea came to me—an idea, big, real."

"Will it deal with her?"

Ernest smiled: "Oh, no. She personally has nothing to do with it. At least not directly. It was the commotion of blood and—brain. The air—the change. I don't know what."

"What will it be?" asked Jack, with interest all alert.

"A play, a wonderful play. And its heroine will be a princess, a little princess, with a yellow veil."

"What of the plot?"

"That I shall not tell you to-day. In fact, I shall not breathe a word to any one. It will take you all by surprise—and the public by storm."

"So it will be playable?"

"If I am not very much mistaken, you will see it on Broadway within a year. And," he added graciously, "I will let you have two box-seats for the first night."

They both chuckled at the thought, and their hearts leaped within them.

"I hope you will finish it soon," Jack observed after a while. "You haven't done much of late."

"A similar reflection was on my mind when you came yesterday. That accounts for the low spirits in which you found me."

"Ah, indeed," Jack replied, measuring Ernest with a look of wonder. "But now your face is aglow. It seems that the blood rushes to your head swifter at the call of an idea than at the kiss of a girl."

"Thank God!" Ernest remarked with a sigh of relief. "Mighty forces within me are fashioning the limpid thought. Passion may grip us by the throat momentarily; upon our backs we may feel the lashes of desire and bathe our souls in flames of many hues; but the joy of activity is the ultimate passion.

Chapter 9

It seemed, indeed, as if work was to Ernest what the sting of pleasure is to the average human animal. The inter-play of his mental forces gave him the sensuous satisfaction of a woman's embrace. His eyes sparkled. His muscle tightened. The joy of creation was upon him.

Often very material reasons, like stone weights tied to the wings of a bird, stayed the flight of his imagination. Magazines were waiting for his copy, and he was not in the position to let them wait. They supplied his bread and butter.

Between the bread and butter, however, the play was growing scene by scene. In the lone hours of the night he spun upon the loom of his fancy a brilliant weft of swift desire—heavy, perfumed, Oriental—interwoven with bits of gruesome tenderness. The thread of his own life intertwined with the thread of the story. All genuine art is autobiography. It is not, however, necessarily a revelation of the artist's actual self, but of a myriad of potential selves. Ah, our own potential selves! They are sometimes beautiful, often horrible, and always fascinating. They loom to heavens none too high for our reach; they stray to yawning hells beneath our very feet.

The man who encompasses heaven and hell is a perfect man. But there are many heavens and more hells. The artist snatches fire from both. Surely the assassin feels no more intensely the lust of murder than the poet who depicts it in glowing words. The things he writes are as real to him as the things that he lives. But in his realm the poet is supreme. His hands may be red with blood or white with leprosy: he still remains king. Woe to him, however, if he transcends the limits of his kingdom and translates into action the secret of his dreams. The throng that before applauded him will stone his quivering body or nail to the cross his delicate hands and feet.

Sometimes days passed before Ernest could concentrate his mind upon his play. Then the fever seized him again, and he strung pearl on pearl, line on line, without entrusting a word to paper.

Even to discuss his work before it had received the final brush-strokes would have seemed indecent to him.

Reginald, too, seemed to be in a turmoil of work. Ernest had little chance to speak to him. And to drop even a hint of his plans between the courses at breakfast would have been desecration.

Sunset followed sunset, night followed night. The stripling April had made room for the lady May. The play was almost completed in Ernest's mind, and he thought, with a little shudder, of the physical travail of the actual writing. He felt that the transcript from brain to paper would demand all his powers. For, of late, his thoughts seemed strangely evanescent; they seemed to run away from him whenever he attempted to seize them.

The day was glad with sunshine, and he decided to take a long walk in the solitude of the Palisades, to steady hand and nerve for the final task.

He told Reginald of his intention, but met with little response. Reginald's face was wan and bore the peculiar pallor of one who had worked late at night.

"You must be frightfully busy?" Ernest asked, with genuine concern.

"So I am," Reginald replied. "I always work in a white heat. I am restless, nervous, feverish, and can find no peace until I have given utterance to all that clamours after birth."

"What is it that is so engaging your mind, the epic of the French Revolution?"

"Oh, no. I should never have undertaken that. I haven't done a stroke of work on it for several weeks. In fact, ever since Walkham called, I simply couldn't. It seemed as if a rough hand had in some way destroyed the web of my thought. Poetry in the writing is like red hot glass before the master-blower has fashioned it into birds and trees and strange fantastic shapes. A draught, caused by the opening of a door may distort it. But at present I am engaged upon more important work. I am modelling a vessel not of fine-spun glass, but of molten gold."

"You make me exceedingly anxious to know what you have in store for us. It seems to me you have reached a point where even you can no longer surpass yourself."

Reginald smiled. "Your praise is too generous, yet it warms like sunshine. I will confess that my conception is unique. It combines with the ripeness of my technique the freshness of a second spring."

Ernest was bubbling with anticipated delights. His soul responded to Reginald's touch as a harp to the winds. "When," he cried, "shall we be privileged to see it?"

Reginald's eyes were already straying back to his writing table. "If the gods are propitious," he remarked, "I shall complete it tonight. To-morrow is my reception, and I have half promised to read it then."

"Perhaps I shall be in the position soon to let you see my play."

"Let us hope so," Reginald replied absentmindedly. The egotism of the artist had once more chained him to his work.

Chapter 10

That night a brilliant crowd had gathered in Reginald Clarke's house. From the studio and the adjoining salon arose a continual murmur of well-tuned voices. On bare white throats jewels shone as if in each a soul were imprisoned, and voluptuously rustled the silk that clung to the fair slim forms of its bearers in an undulating caress. Subtle perfumes emanated from the hair and the hands of syren women, commingling with the soft plump scent of their flesh. Fragrant tapers, burning in precious crystal globules stained with exquisite colours, sprinkled their shimmering

light over the fashionable assemblage and lent a false radiance to the faces of the men, while in the hair and the jewels of the women each ray seemed to dance like an imp with its mate.

A seat like a throne, covered with furs of tropic beasts of prey, stood in one corner of the room in the full glare of the light, waiting for the monarch to come. Above were arranged with artistic raffinement weird oriental draperies, resembling a crimson canopy in the total effect. Chattering visitors were standing in groups, or had seated themselves on the divans and curiously-fashioned chairs that were scattered in seeming disorder throughout the salon. There were critics and writers and men of the world. Everybody who was anybody and a little bigger than somebody else was holding court in his own small circle of enthusiastic admirers. The Bohemian element was subdued, but not entirely lacking. The magic of Reginald Clarke's name made stately dames blind to the presence of some individuals whom they would have passed on the street without recognition.

Ernest surveyed this gorgeous assembly with the absent look of a sleep-walker. Not that his sensuous soul was unsusceptible to the atmosphere of culture and corruption that permeated the whole, nor to the dazzling colour effects that tantalised while they delighted the eye. But to-night they shrivelled into insignificance before the splendour of his inner vision. A radiant dreamland palace, his play, had risen from the night of inchoate thought. It was wonderful, it was real, and needed for its completion only the detail of actual construction. And now the characters were hovering in the recesses of his brain, were yearning to leave that many-winded labyrinth to become real beings of paper and ink. He would probably have tarried overlong in this fanciful mansion, had not the reappearance of an unexpected guest broken his reverie.

"Jack!" he exclaimed in surprise, "I thought you a hundred miles away from here."

"That shows that you no longer care for me," Jack playfully answered. "When our friendship was young, you always had a presentiment of my presence."

"Ah, perhaps I had. But tell me, where do you hail from?"

"Clarke called me up on the telephone—long-distance, you know. I suppose it was meant as a surprise for you. And you certainly looked surprised—not even pleasantly. I am really head- over-heels at work. But you know how it is. Sometimes a little imp whispers into my ears daring me to do a thing which I know is foolish. But what of it? My legs are strong enough not to permit my follies to overtake me."

"It was certainly good of you to come. In fact, you make me very glad. I feel that I need you to-night—I don't know why. The feeling came suddenly—suddenly as you. I only know I need you. How long can you stay?"

"I must leave you to-morrow morning. I have to hustle somewhat. You know my examinations are taking place in a day or two and I've got to cram up a lot of things."

"Still," remarked Ernest, "your visit will repay you for the loss of time. Clarke will read to us to-night his masterpiece."

"What is it?"

"I don't know. I only know it's the real thing. It's worth all the wisdom bald-headed professors may administer to you in concentrated doses at five thousand a year."

"Come now," Jack could not help saying, "is your memory giving way? Don't you remember your own days in college—especially the mathematical examinations? You know that your marks came always pretty near the absolute zero."

"Jack," cried Ernest in honest indignation, "not the last time. The last time I didn't flunk."

"No, because your sonnet on Cartesian geometry roused even the math-fiend to compassion. And don't you remember Professor Squeeler, whose heart seemed to leap with delight whenever

he could tell you that, in spite of incessant toil on your part, he had again flunked you in physics with fifty-nine and a half per cent.?"

"And he wouldn't raise the mark to sixty I God forgive him,—I cannot." Here their exchange of reminiscences was interrupted. There was a stir. The little potentates of conversation hastened to their seats, before their minions had wholly deserted them.

The king was moving to his throne!

Assuredly Reginald Clarke had the bearing of a king. Leisurely he took his seat under the canopy.

A hush fell on the audience; not a fan stirred as he slowly unfolded his manuscript.

Chapter 11

The music of Reginald Clarke's intonation captivated every ear. Voluptuously, in measured cadence, it rose and fell; now full and strong like the sound of an organ, now soft and clear like the tinkling of bells. His voice detracted by its very tunefulness from what he said. The powerful spell charmed even Ernest's accustomed ear. The first page gracefully glided from Reginald's hand to the carpet before the boy dimly realised that he was intimately familiar with every word that fell from Reginald's lips. When the second page slipped with seeming carelessness from the reader's hand, a sudden shudder ran through the boy's frame. It was as if an icy hand had gripped his heart. There could be no doubt of it. This was more than mere coincidence. It was plagiarism. He wanted to cry out.

But the room swam before his eyes.

Surely he must be dreaming. It was a dream. The faces of the audience, the lights, Reginald, jack—all phantasmagoria of a dream.

Perhaps he had been ill for a long time. Perhaps Clarke was reading the play for him. He did not remember having written it. But he probably had fallen sick after its completion. What strange pranks our memories will play us! But no! He was not dreaming, and he had not been ill.

He could endure the horrible uncertainty no longer. His overstrung nerves must find relaxation in some way or break with a twang. He turned to his friend who was listening with rapt attention.

"Jack, Jack!" he whispered. "What is it?"

"That is my play!"

"You mean that you inspired it?"

"No, I have written it, or rather, was going to write it. "Wake up, Ernest! You are mad!"

"No, in all seriousness. It is mine. I told you—don't you remember—when we returned from Coney Island—that I was writing a play."

"Ah, but not this play."

"Yes, this play. I conceived it, I practically wrote it."

"The more's the pity that Clarke had preconceived it."

"But it is mine !"

"Did you tell him a word about it?"

"No, to be sure."

"Did you leave the manuscript in your room?"

"I had, in fact, not written a line of it. No, I had not begun the actual writing."

"Why should a man of Clarke's reputation plagiarise your plays, written or unwritten?"

"I can see no reason. But—"

"Tut, tut."

For already this whispered conversation had elicited a look like a stab from a lady before them. Ernest held fast td the edge of a chair. He must cling to some reality, or else drift rudderless in a dim sea of vague apprehensions.

Or was Jack right?

Was his mind giving way? No! No! No! There must be a monstrous secret somewhere, but what matter? Did anything matter? He had called on his mate like a ship lost in the fog. For the first time he had not responded. He had not understood. The bitterness of tears rose to the boy's eyes.

Above it all, melodiously, ebbed and flowed the rich accents of Reginald Clarke. Ernest listened to the words of his own play coming from the older man's mouth. The horrible fascination of the scene held him entranced. He saw the creations of his mind pass in review before him, as a man might look upon the face of his double grinning at him from behind a door in the hideous hours of night.

They were all there! The mad king. The subtle-witted courtiers. The sombre-hearted Prince. The Queen-Mother who had loved a jester better than her royal mate, and the fruit of their shameful alliance, the Princess Marigold, a creature woven of sunshine and sin.

Swiftly the action progressed. Shadows of impending death darkened the house of the King. In the horrible agony of the rack the old jester confessed. Stripped of his cap and bells, crowned with a wreath of blood, he looked so pathetically funny that the Princess Marigold could not help laughing between her tears.

The Queen stood there all trembling and pale. Without a complaint she saw her lover die. The executioner's sword smote the old man's head straight from the trunk. It rolled at the feet of the King, who tossed it to Marigold. The little Princess kissed it and covered the grinning horror with her yellow veil.

The last words died away.

There was no applause. Only silence. All were stricken with the dread that men feel in the house of God or His awful presence in genius.

But the boy lay back in his chair. The cold sweat had gathered on his brow and his temples throbbed. Nature had mercifully clogged his head with blood. The rush of it drowned the crying voice of the nerves, deadening for a while both consciousness and pain.

Chapter 12

Somehow the night had passed—somehow in bitterness, in anguish. But it had passed.

Ernest's lips were parched and sleeplessness had left its trace in the black rings under the eyes, when the next morning he confronted Reginald in the studio.

Reginald was sitting at the writing-table in his most characteristic pose, supporting his head with his hand and looking with clear piercing eyes searchingly at the boy.

"Yes," he observed, "it's a most curious psychical phenomenon."

"You cannot imagine how real it all seemed to me."

The boy spoke painfully, dazed, as if struck by a blow.

"Even now it is as if something has gone from me, some struggling thought that I cannot— cannot remember."

Reginald regarded him as a physical experimenter might look upon the subject of a particularly baffling mental disease.

"You must not think, my boy, that I bear you any malice for your extraordinary delusion. Before Jack went away he gave me an exact account of all that has happened. Divers incidents recurred to him from which it appears that, at various times in the past, you have been on the verge of a nervous collapse."

A nervous collapse! What was the use of this term but a euphemism for insanity?

"Do not despair, dear child," Reginald caressingly remarked. "Your disorder is not hopeless, not incurable. Such crises come to every man who writes. It is the tribute we pay to the Lords of Song. The minnesinger of the past wrote with his heart's blood; but we moderns dip our pen into the sap of our nerves. We analyse life, love art—and the dissecting knife that we use on other men's souls finally turns against ourselves.

"But what shall a man do? Shall he sacrifice art to hygiene and surrender the one attribute that makes him chiefest of created things? Animals, too, think. Some walk on two legs. But introspection differentiates man from the rest. Shall we yield up the sweet consciousness of self that we derive from the analysis of our emotion, for the contentment of the bull that ruminates in the shade of a tree or the healthful stupidity of a mule?"

"Assuredly not."

"But what shall a man do?"

"Ah, that I cannot tell. Mathematics offers definite problems that admit of a definite solution. Life states its problems with less exactness and offers for each a different solution. One and one are two to-day and to-morrow. Psychical values, on each manipulation, will yield a different result. Still, your case is quite clear. You have overworked yourself in the past, mentally and emotionally. You have sown unrest, and must not be surprised if neurasthenia is the harvest thereof."

"Do you think—that I should go to some sanitarium?" the boy falteringly asked.

"God forbid! Go to the seashore, somewhere where you can sleep and play. Take your body along, but leave your brain behind—at least do not take more of it with you than is necessary. The summer season in Atlantic City has just begun. There, as everywhere in American society, you will be much more welcome if you come without brains."

Reginald's half-bantering tone reassured Ernest a little. Timidly he dared approach once more the strange event that had wrought such havoc with his nervous equilibrium.

"How do you account for my strange obsession—one might almost call it a mania?"

"If it could be accounted for it would not be strange."

"Can you suggest no possible explanation?"

"Perhaps a stray leaf on my desk a few indications of the plot, a remark—who knows? Perhaps thought-matter is floating in the air. Perhaps—but we had better not talk of it now. It would needlessly excite you."

"You are right," answered Ernest gloomily, "let us not talk of it. But whatever may be said, it is a marvellous play."

"You flatter me. There is nothing in it that you may not be able to do equally well—some day."

"Ah, no," the boy replied, looking up to Reginald with admiration. "You are the master."

Chapter 13

Lazily Ernest stretched his limbs on the beach of Atlantic City. The sea, that purger of sick souls, had washed away the fever and the fret of the last few days. The wind was in his hair and the spray was in his breath, while the rays of the sun kissed his bare arms and legs. He rolled over in the glittering sand in the sheer joy of living.

Now and then a wavelet stole far into the beach, as if to caress him, but pined away ere it could reach its goal. It was as if the enamoured sea was stretching out its arms to him. Who knows, perhaps through the clear water some green-eyed nymph, or a young sea-god with the tang of the sea in his hair, was peering amorously at the boy's red mouth. The people of the deep love the red warm blood of human kind. It is always the young that they lure to their watery haunts, never the shrivelled limbs that totter shivering to the grave.

Such fancies came to Ernest as he lay on the shore in his bathing attire, happy, thoughtless,— animal.

The sun and the sea seemed to him two lovers vying for his favor. The sudden change of environment had brought complete relaxation and had quieted his rebellious, assertive soul. He was no longer a solitary unit but one with wind and water, herb and beach and shell. Almost voluptuously his hand toyed with the hot sand that glided caressingly through his fingers and buried his breast and shoulder under its glittering burden.

A summer girl who passed lowered her eyes coquettishly. He watched her without stirring. Even to open his mouth or to smile would have seemed too much exertion.

Thus he lay for hours. When at length noon drew nigh, it cost him a great effort of will to shake off his drowsy mood and exchange his airy costume for the conventional habilaments of the dining-room.

He had taken lodgings in a fashionable hotel. An unusual stroke of good luck, hack-work that paid outrageously well, had made it possible for him to idle for a time without a thought of the unpleasant necessity of making money.

One single article to which he signed his name only with reluctance had brought to him more gear than a series of golden sonnets.

"Surely," he thought, "the social revolution ought to begin from above. What right has the bricklayer to grumble when he receives for a week's work almost more than I for a song?"

Thus soliloquising, he reached the dining-room. The scene that unfolded itself before him was typical—the table over-loaded, the women over-dressed.

The luncheon was already in full course when he came. He mumbled an apology and seated himself on the only remaining chair next to a youth who reminded him of a well-dressed dummy. With slight weariness his eyes wandered in all directions for more congenial faces when they were arrested by a lady on the opposite side of the table. She was clad in a silk robe with curiously embroidered net-work that revealed a nervous and delicate throat. The rich effect of the net-work was relieved by the studied simplicity with which her heavy chestnut-colored hair was gathered in a single knot. Her face was turned away from him, but there was something in the carriage of her head that struck him as familiar. When at last she looked him in the face, the glass almost fell from his hand: it was Ethel Brandenbourg. She seemed to notice his embarrassment and smiled. When she opened her lips to speak, he knew by the haunting sweetness of the voice that he was not mistaken.

"Tell me," she said wistfully, "you have forgotten me? They all have."

He hastened to assure her that he had not forgotten her. He recollected now that he had first been introduced to her in Walkham's house some years ago, when a mere college boy, he had been privileged to attend one of that master's famous receptions. She had looked quite resolute and very happy then, not at all like the woman who had stared so strangely at Reginald in the Broadway restaurant.

He regarded this encounter as very fortunate. He knew so much of her personal history that it almost seemed to him as if they had been intimate for years. She, too, felt on familiar ground with him. Neither as much as whispered the name of Reginald Clarke. Yet it was he, and the knowledge of what he was to them, that linked their souls with a common bond.

Chapter 14

It was the third day after their meeting. Hour by hour their intimacy had increased. Ethel was sitting in a large wicker-chair. She restlessly fingered her parasol, mechanically describing magic circles in the sand. Ernest lay at her feet. With his knees clasped between his hands, he gazed into her eyes.

"Why are you trying so hard to make love to me?" the woman asked, with the half-amused smile with which the Eve near thirty receives the homage of a boy. There is an element of insincerity in that smile, but it is a weapon of defence against love's artillery.

Sometimes, indeed, the pleading in the boy's eyes and the cry of the blood pierces the woman's smiling superiority. She listens, loves and loses.

Ethel Brandenbourg was listening, but the idea of love had not yet entered into her mind. Her interest in Ernest was due in part to his youth and the trembling in his voice when he spoke of love. But what probably attracted her most powerfully was the fact that he intimately knew the man who still held her woman's heart in the hollow of his hand. It was half in play, therefore, that she had asked him that question.

Why did he make love to her? He did not know. Perhaps it was the irresistible desire to be petted which young poets share with domesticated cats. But what should he tell her? Polite platitudes were out of place between them.

Besides he knew the penalty of all tender entanglements. Women treat love as if it were an extremely tenuous wire that can be drawn out indefinitely. This is a very expensive process. It costs us the most precious, the only irretrievable thing in the universe—time. And to him time was song; for money he did not care. The Lord had hallowed his lips with rhythmic speech; only in the intervals of his singing might he listen to the voice of his heart—strangest of all watches, that tells the time not by minutes and hours, but by the coming and going of love.

The woman beside him seemed to read his thoughts.

"Child, child," she said, "why will you toy with love? Like Jehovah, he is a jealous god, and nothing but the whole heart can placate him. Woe to the woman who takes a poet for a lover. I admit it is fascinating, but it is playing va banque. In fact, it is fatal. Art or love will come to harm. No man can minister equally to both. A genuine poet is incapable of loving a woman."

"Pshaw! You exaggerate. Of course, there is a measure of truth in what you say, but it is only one side of the truth, and the truth, you know, is always Janus-faced. In fact, it often has more than two faces. I can assure you that I have cared deeply for the women to whom my love-poetry was written. And you will not deny that it is genuine."

"God forbid! Only you have been using the wrong preposition. You should have said that it was written at them."

Ernest stared at her in child-like wonder.

"By Jove! you are too devilishly clever!" he exclaimed. After a little silence he said not without hesitation: "And do you apply your theory to all artists, or only to us makers of rhyme?"

"To all," she replied.

He looked at her questioningly.

"Yes," she said, with a new sadness in her voice, "I, too, have paid the price."

"You mean?"

"I loved."

"And art?"

"That was the sacrifice."

"Perhaps you have chosen the better part," Ernest said without conviction.

"No," she replied, "my tribute was brought in vain."

This she said calmly, but Ernest knew that her words were of tragic import. "You love him still?" he observed simply. Ethel made no reply. Sadness clouded her face like a veil or like a grey mist over the face of the waters. Her eyes went out to the sea, following the sombre flight of the sea-mews.

In that moment he could have taken her in his arms and kissed her with infinite tenderness. But tenderness between man and woman is like a match in a powder-magazine. The least provocation, and an amorous explosion will ensue, tumbling down the card-houses of platonic affection. If he yielded to the impulse of the moment, the wine of the springtide would set their blood afire, and from the flames within us there is no escape.

"Come, come," she said, "you do not love me."

He protested.

"Ah!" she cried triumphantly, "how many sonnets would you give for me? If you were a usurer in gold instead of in rhyme, I would ask how many dollars. But it is unjust to pay in a coin that we value little. To a man starving in gold mines, a piece of bread weighs more than all the treasures of the earth. To you, I warrant your poems are the standard of appreciation. How many would you give for me? One, two, three?

"More."

"Because you think love would repay you with compound interest," she observed merrily. He laughed.

And when love turns to laughter the danger is passed for the moment.

Chapter 15

Thus three weeks passed without apparent change in their relations. Ernest possessed a personal magnetism that, always emanating from him, was felt most deeply when withdrawn. He was at all times involuntarily exerting his power, which she ever resisted, always on the alert, always warding off.

When at last pressure of work made his immediate departure for New York imperative, he had not apparently gained the least ground. But Ethel knew in her heart that she was fascinated, if not in love. The personal fascination was supplemented by a motherly feeling toward Ernest that, sensuous in essence, was in itself not far removed from love. She struggled bravely and with external success against her emotions, never losing sight of the fact that twenty and thirty are fifty.

Increasingly aware of her own weakness, she constantly attempted to lead the conversation into impersonal channels, speaking preferably of his work.

"Tell me," she said, negligently fanning herself, "what new inspiration have you drawn from your stay at the seaside?"

"Why," he exclaimed enthusiastically, "volumes and volumes of it. I shall write the great novel of my life after I am once more quietly installed at Riverside Drive."

"The great American novel?" she rejoined. "Perhaps."

"Who will be your hero—Clarke?"

"There was a slight touch of malice in her words, or rather in the pause between the penultimate word and the last. Ernest detected its presence, and knew that her love for Reginald was dead. Stiff and cold it lay in her heart's chamber—beside how many others?—all emboxed in the coffin of memory.

"No," he replied after a while, a little piqued by her suggestion, "Clarke is not the hero. What makes you think that he casts a spell on everything I do?"

"Dear child," she replied, "I know him.

He cannot fail to impress his powerful personality upon all with whom he comes in contact, to the injury of their intellectual independence. Moreover, he is so brilliant and says everything so much better than anybody else, that by his very splendor he discourages effort in others. At best his influence will shape your development according to the tenets of his mind—curious, subtle and corrupted. You will become mentally distorted, like one of those hunchback Japanese trees, infinitely wrinkled and infinitely grotesque, whose laws of growth are not determined by nature, but by the diseased imagination of the East."

"I am no weakling," Ernest asserted, "and your picture of Clarke is altogether out of perspective. His splendid successes are to me a source of constant inspiration. We have some things in common, but I realise that it is along entirely different lines that success will come to me. He has never sought to influence me, in fact, I never received the smallest suggestion from him." Here the Princess Marigold seemed to peer at him through the veil of the past, but he waved her aside. "As for my story," he continued, "you need not go so far out of your way to find the leading character?"

"Who can it be?" Ethel remarked, with a merry twinkle, "You?"

"Ethel," he said sulkingly, "be serious. You know that it is you."

"I am immensely flattered," she replied. "Really, nothing pleases me better than to be immortalised in print, since I have little hope nowadays of perpetuating my name by virtue of pencil or brush. I have been put into novels before and am consumed with curiosity to hear the plot of yours."

"If you don't mind, I had rather not tell you just yet," Ernest said. "It's going to be called Leontina—that's you. But all depends on the treatment. You know it doesn't matter much what you say so long as you say it well. That's what counts. At any rate, any indication of the plot at this stage would be decidedly inadequate."

"I think you are right," she ventured. "By all means choose your own time to tell me. Let's talk of something else. Have you written anything since your delightful book of verse last spring? Surely now is your singing season. By the time we are thirty the springs of pure lyric passion are usually exhausted."

Ethel's inquiry somehow startled him. In truth, he could find no satisfactory answer. A remark relative to his play—Clarke's play— rose to the threshold of his lips, but he almost bit his tongue

as soon as he realised that the strange delusion which had possessed him that night still dominated the undercurrents of his cerebration. No, he had accomplished but little during the last few months—at least, by way of creative literature. So he replied that he had made money. "That is something," he said. "Besides, who can turn out a masterpiece every week? An artist's brain is not a machine, and in the respite from creative work I have gathered strength for the future. But," he added, slightly annoyed, "you are not listening."

His exclamation brought her back from the train of thoughts that his words had suggested. For in his reasoning she had recognised the same arguments that she had hourly repeated to herself in defence of her inactivity when she was living under the baneful influence of Reginald Clarke. Yes, baneful; for the first time she dared to confess it to herself. In a flash the truth dawned upon her that it was not her love alone, but something else, something irresistable and very mysterious, that had dried up the well of creation in her. Could it be that the same power was now exerting its influence upon the struggling soul of this talented boy? Rack her brains as she might, she could not definitely formulate her apprehensions and a troubled look came into her eyes.

"Ethel," the boy repeated, impatiently, "why are you not listening? Do you realise that I must leave you in half an hour?"

She looked at him with deep tenderness. Something like a tear lent a soft radiance to her large child-like eyes.

Ernest saw it and was profoundly moved. In that moment he loved her passionately.

"Foolish boy," she said softly; then, lowering her voice to a whisper: "You may kiss me before you go."

His lips gently touched hers, but she took his head between her hands and pressed her mouth upon his in a long kiss.

Ernest drew back a little awkwardly. He had not been kissed like this before.

"Poet though you are," Ethel whispered, "you have not yet learned to kiss." She was deeply agitated when she noticed that his hand was fumbling for the watch in his vest- pocket. She suddenly released him, and said, a little hurt: "No, you must not miss your train. Go by all means."

Vainly Ernest remonstrated with her. "Go to him," she said, and again, "go to him," With a heavy heart the boy obeyed. He waved his hat to her once more from below, and then rapidly disappeared in the crowd. For a moment strange misgivings cramped her heart, and something within her called out to him: "Do not go! Do not return to that house." But no sound issued from her lips. Worldly wisdom had sealed them, had stifled the inner voice. And soon the boy's golden head was swallowed up in the distance.

Chapter 16

While the train sped to New York, Ethel Brandenbourg was the one object engaging Ernest's mind. He still felt the pressure of her lips upon his, and his nostrils dilated at the thought of the fragrance of her hair brushing against his forehead.

But the moment his foot touched the ferryboat that was to take him to Manhattan, the past three weeks were, for the time being at least, completely obliterated from his memory. All his other interests that he had suppressed in her company because she had no part in them, came rushing back to him. He anticipated with delight his meeting with Reginald Clarke. The personal attractiveness of the man had never seemed so powerful to Ernest as when he had not heard from

him for some time. Reginald's letters were always brief. "Professional writers," he was wont to say, "cannot afford to put fine feeling into their private correspondence. They must turn it into copy:' He longed to sit with the master in the studio when the last rays of the daylight were tremulously falling through the stained window, and to discuss far into the darkening night philosophies young and old. He longed for Reginald's voice, his little mannerisms, the very perfume of his rooms.

There also was a deluge of letters likely to await him in his apartment. For in his hurried departure he had purposely left his friends in the dark as to his whereabouts. Only to Jack he had dropped a little note the day after his meeting with Ethel.

He earnestly hoped to find Reginald at home, though it was well nigh ten o'clock in the evening, and he cursed the "rapid transit" for its inability to annihilate space and time. It is indeed disconcerting to think how many months, if not years, of our earthly sojourn the dwellers in cities spend in transportation conveyances that must be set down as a dead loss in the ledger of life. A nervous impatience against things material overcame Ernest in the subway. It is ever the mere stupid obstacle of matter that weights down the wings of the soul and prevents it from soaring upward to the sun.

When at last he had reached the house, he learned from the hall-boy that Clarke had gone out. Ruffled in temper he entered his rooms and went over his mail. There were letters from editors with commissions that he could not afford to reject. Everywhere newspapers and magazines opened their yawning mouths to swallow up what time he had. He realised at once that he would have to postpone the writing of his novel for several weeks, if not longer.

Among the letters was one from Jack. It bore the postmark of a little place in the Adirondacks where he was staying with his parents. Ernest opened the missive not without hesitation. On reading and rereading it the fine lines on his forehead, that would some day deepen into wrinkles, became quite pronounced and a look of displeasure darkened his face. Something was wrong with Jack, a slight change that defied analysis. Their souls were out of tune. It might only be a passing disturbance; perhaps it was his own fault. It pained him, nevertheless. Somehow it seemed of late that Jack was no longer able to follow the vagaries of his mind. Only one person in the world possessed a similar mental vision, only one seemed to understand what he said and what he left unsaid. Reginald Clarke, being a man and poet, read in his soul as in an open book. Ethel might have understood, had not love, like a cloud, laid itself between her eyes and the page.

It was with exultation that Ernest heard near midnight the click of Reginald's key in the door. He found him unchanged, completely, radiantly himself. Reginald possessed the psychic power of undressing the soul, of seeing it before him in primal nakedness. Although no word was said of Ethel Brandenbourg except the mere mention of her presence in Atlantic City, Ernest intuitively knew that Reginald was aware of the transformation that absence had wrought in him. In the presence of this man he could be absolutely himself, without shame or fear of misunderstanding; and by a strange metamorphosis, all his affection for Ethel and Jack went out for the time being to Reginald Clarke.

Chapter 17

The next day Ernest wrote a letter of more or less superficial tenderness to Ethel. She had wounded his pride by proving victorious in the end over his passion and hers; besides, he was in the throes of work. When after the third day no answer came, he was inclined to feel aggrieved.

It was plain now that she had not cared for him in the least, but had simply played with him for lack of another toy. A flush of shame rose to his cheeks at the thought. He began to analyse his own emotions, and stunned, if not stabbed, his passion step by step. Work was calling to him. It was that which gave life its meaning, not the love of a season. How far away, how unreal, she now seemed to him. Yes, she was right, he had not cared deeply; and his novel, too, would be written only at her. It was the heroine of his story that absorbed his interest, not the living prototype.

Once in a conversation with Reginald he touched upon the subject. Reginald held that modern taste no longer permitted even the photographer to portray life as it is, but insisted upon an individual visualisation. "No man," he remarked, "was ever translated bodily into fiction. In contradiction to life, art is a process of artificial selection."

Bearing in mind this motive, Ernest went to work to mould from the material in hand a new Ethel, more real than life. Unfortunately he found little time to devote to his novel. It was only when, after a good day's work, a pile of copy for a magazine lay on his desk, that he could think of concentrating his mind upon "Leontina." The result was that when he went to bed his imagination was busy with the plan of his book, and the creatures of his own brain laid their fingers on his eyelid so that he could not sleep.

When at last sheer weariness overcame him, his mind was still at work, not in orderly sequence but along trails monstrous and grotesque. Hobgoblins seemed to steal through the hall, and leering incubi oppressed his soul with terrible burdens. In the morning he awoke unrested. The tan vanished from his face and little lines appeared in the corners of his mouth. It was as if his nervous vitality were sapped from him in some unaccountable way. He became excited, hysterical. Often at night when he wrote his pot-boilers for the magazines, fear stood behind his seat, and only the buzzing of the elevator outside brought him back to himself.

In one of his morbid moods he wrote a sonnet which he showed to Reginald after the latter's return from a short trip out of town. Reginald read it, looking at the boy with a curious, lurking expression.

> *O gentle Sleep, turn not thy face away,*
> *But place thy finger on my brow, and take*
>
> *All burthens from me and all dreams that ache,*
>
> *Upon mine eyes a cooling balsam lay,*
>
> *Seeing I am aweary of the day.*
>
> *But, lo! thy lips are ashen and they quake.*
>
> *What spectral vision sees thou that can shake*
>
> *Thy sweet composure, and thy heart dismay?*
>
> *Perhaps some murderer's cruel eye agleam*
>
> *Is fixed upon me, or some monstrous dream*
>
> *Might bring such fearful guilt upon the head*
>
> *Of my unvigilant soul as would arouse*
>
> *The Borgian snake from her envenomed bed,*
>
> *Or startle Nero in his golden house.*

"Good stuff," Reginald remarked, laying down the manuscript; "when did you write it?' "The night when you were out of town," Ernest rejoined.

"I see," Reginald replied.

There was something startling in his intonation that at once aroused Ernest's attention. "What do you see?" he asked quickly.

"Nothing," Reginald replied, with immovable calm, "only that your state of nerves is still far from satisfactory."

Chapter 18

After Ernest's departure Ethel Brandenbourg's heart was swaying hither and thither in a hurricane of conflicting feelings. Before she had time to gain an emotional equilibrium, his letter had hurled her back into chaos. A false ring somewhere in Ernest's words, reechoing with an ever-increasing volume of sound, stifled the voice of love. His jewelled sentences glittered, but left her cold. They lacked that spontaneity which renders even simple and hackeneyed phrases wonderful and unique. Ethel clearly realised that her hold upon the boy's imagination had been a fleeting midsummer night's charm, and that a word from Reginald's lips had broken the potency of her spell. She almost saw the shadow of Reginald's visage hovering over Ernest's letter and leering at her from between the lines in sinister triumph. Finally reason came and whispered to her that it was extremely unwise to give her heart into the keeping of a boy. His love, she knew, would have been exacting, irritating at times. He would have asked her to sympathise with every phase of his life, and would have expected active interest on her part in much that she had done with long ago. Thus, untruth would have stolen into her life and embittered it. When mates are unequal, Love must paint its cheeks and, in certain moods at least, hide its face under a mask. Its lips may be honeyed, but it brings fret and sorrow in its train.

These things she told herself over and over again while she penned a cool and calculating answer to Ernest's letter. She rewrote it many times, and every time it became more difficult to reply. At last she put her letter aside for a few days, and when it fell again into her hand it seemed so unnatural and strained that she destroyed it.

Thus several weeks had passed, and Ernest no longer exclusively occupied her mind when, one day early in September, while glancing over a magazine, she came upon his name in the table of contents. Once more she saw the boy's wistful face before her, and a trembling something stirred in her heart. Her hand shook as she cut the pages, and a mist of tears clouded her vision as she attempted to read his poem. It was a piece of sombre brilliance. Like black-draped monks half crazed with mystic devotion, the poet's thoughts flitted across the page. It was the wail of a soul that feels reason slipping from it and beholds madness rise over its life like a great pale moon. A strange unrest emanated from it and took possession of her. And again, with an insight that was prophetic, she distinctly recognised behind the vague fear that had haunted the poet the figure of Reginald Clarke.

A half-forgotten dream, struggling to consciousness, staggered her by its vividness. She saw Clarke as she had seen him in days gone by, grotesquely transformed into a slimy seathing, whose hungry mouths shut sucking upon her and whose thousand tentacles encircled her form. She closed her eyes in horror at the reminiscence. And in that moment it became clear to her that she must take into her hands the salvation of Ernest Fielding from the clutches of the malign power that had mysteriously enveloped his life.

Chapter 19

The summer was brief, and already by the middle of September many had returned to the pleasures of urban life. Ethel was among the first-comers; for, after her resolve to enter the life of the young poet once more, it would have been impossible for her to stay away from the city

much longer. Her plan was all ready. Before attempting to see Ernest she would go to meet Reginald and implore him to free the boy from his hideous spell. An element of curiosity unconsciously entered her determination. When, years ago, she and Clarke had parted, the man had seemed, for once, greatly disturbed and had promised, in his agitation, that some day he would communicate to her what would exonerate him in her eyes. She had answered that all words between them were purposeless, and that she hoped never to see his face again. The experience that the years had brought to her, instead of elucidating the mystery of Reginald's personality, had, on the contrary, made his behaviour appear more and more unaccountable. She had more than once caught herself wishing to meet him again and to analyse dispassionately the puzzling influences he had exerted upon her. And she could at last view him dispassionately; there was triumph in that. She was dimly aware that something had passed from her, something by which he had held her, and without which his magnetism was unable to play upon her.

So when Walkham sent her an invitation to one of his artistic "at homes" she accepted, in. the hope of meeting Reginald. It was his frequentation of Walkham's house that had for several years effectively barred her foot from crossing the threshold. It was with a very strange feeling she greeted the many familiar faces at Walkham's now; and when, toward ten o'clock, Reginald entered, politely bowing in answer to the welcome from all sides, her heart beat in her like a drum. But she calmed herself, and, catching his eye, so arranged it that early in the evening they met in an alcove of the drawing-room.

"It was inevitable," Reginald said. "I expected it."

"Yes," she replied, "we were bound to meet." Like a great rush of water, memory came back to her. He was still horribly fascinating as of old—only she was no longer susceptible to his fascination. He had changed somewhat in those years. The lines about his mouth had grown harder and a steel-like look had come into his eyes. Only for a moment, as he looked at her, a flash of tenderness seemed to come back to them. Then he said, with a touch of sadness: "Why should the first word between us be a lie?"

Ethel made no answer.

Reginald looked at her half in wonder and said: "And is your love for the boy so great that it overcame your hate of me?"

Ah, he knew! She winced. "He has told you?"

"Not a word."

There was something superhuman in his power of penetration. Why should she wear a mask before him, when his eyes, like the eyes of God, pierced to the core of her being?

"No," she replied, "it is not love, but compassion for him."

"Compassion?"

"Yes, compassion for your victim."

"You mean?"

"Reginald!"

"I am all ear."

"I implore you."

"Speak."

"You have ruined one life."

He raised his eyebrows derogatively.

"Yes," she continued fiercely, "ruined it! Is not that enough?"

"I have never wilfully ruined any one's life."

"You have ruined mine."

"Wilfully?"

"How else shall I explain your conduct?"

"I warned you."

"Warning, indeed! The warning that the snake gives to the sparrow helpless under its gaze."

"Ah, but who tells you that the snake is to blame? Is it not rather the occult power that prescribes with blood on brazen scroll the law of our being?"

"This is no solace to the sparrow. But whatever may be said, let us drop the past. Let us consider the present. I beg of you, leave this boy—let him develop without your attempting to stifle the life in him or impressing upon it the stamp of your alien mind."

"Ethel," he protested, "you are unjust. If you knew—" Then an idea seemed to take hold of him. He looked at her curiously.

"What if I knew?" she asked.

"You shall know," he said, simply. "Are you strong?"

"Strong to withstand anything at your hand. There is nothing that you can give me, nothing that you can take away."

"No," he remarked, "nothing. Yes, you have changed. Still, when I look upon you, the ghosts of the past seem to rise like live things."

"We both have changed. We meet now upon equal grounds. You are no longer the idol I made of you."

"Don't you think that to the idol this might be a relief, not a humiliation? It is a terrible torture to sit in state with lips eternally shut. Sometimes there comes over the most reticent of us a desire to break through the eternal loneliness that surrounds the soul. It is this feeling that prompts madmen to tear off their clothes and exhibit their nakedness in the market-place. It's madness on my part, or a whim, or I don't know what; but it pleases me that you should know the truth."

"You promised me long ago that I should."

"To-day I will redeem my promise, and I will tell you another thing that you will find hard to believe."

"And that is?"

"That I loved you."

Ethel smiled a little sceptically. "You have loved often."

"No," he replied. "Loved, seriously loved, I have, only once."

Chapter 20

They were sitting in a little Italian restaurant where they had often, in the old days, lingered late into the night over a glass of Lacrimæ Christi. But no pale ghost of the past rose from the wine. Only a wriggling something, with serpent eyes, that sent cold shivers down her spine and held her speechless and entranced.

When their order had been filled and the waiter had posted himself at a respectful distance, Reginald began—at first leisurely, a man of the world. But as he proceeded a strange exultation seemed to possess him and from his eyes leaped the flame of the mystic.

"You must pardon me," he commenced, "if I monopolise the conversation, but the revelations I have to make are of such a nature that I may well claim your attention. I will start with my earliest childhood. You remember the picture of me that was taken when I was five?"

She remembered, indeed. Each detail of his life was deeply engraven on her mind.

"At that time," he continued, "I was not held to be particularly bright. The reason was that my mind, being pre-eminently and extraordinarily receptive, needed a stimulus from without. The moment I was sent to school, however, a curious metamorphosis took place in me. I may say that I became at once the most brilliant boy in my class. You know that to this day I have always been the most striking figure in any circle in which I have ever moved."

Ethel nodded assent. Silently watching the speaker, she saw a gleam of the truth from afar, but still very distant and very dim.

Reginald lifted the glass against the light and gulped its contents. Then in a lower voice he recommenced: "Like the chameleon, I have the power of absorbing the colour of my environment."

"Do you mean that you have the power of absorbing the special virtues of other people?" she interjected.

"That is exactly what I mean."

"Oh!" she cried, for in a heart-beat many things had become clear to her. For the first time she realised, still vaguely but with increasing vividness, the hidden causes of her ruin and, still more plainly, the horrible danger of Ernest Fielding.

He noticed her agitation, and a look of psychological curiosity came into his eyes.

"Ah, but that is not all," he observed, smilingly. "That is nothing. We all possess that faculty in a degree. The secret of my strength is my ability to reject every element that is harmful or inessential to the completion of myself. This did not come to me easily, nor without a struggle. But now, looking back upon my life, many things become transparent that were obscure even to me at the time. I can now follow the fine-spun threads in the intricate web of my fate, and discover in the wilderness of meshes a design, awful and grandly planned."

His voice shook with conviction, as he uttered these words. There was something strangely gruesome in this man. It was thus that she had pictured to herself the high-priest of some terrible and mysterious religion, demanding a human sacrifice to appease the hunger of his god. She was fascinated by the spell of his personality, and listened with a feeling not far removed from awe. But Reginald suddenly changed his tone and proceeded in a more conversational manner.

"The first friend I ever cared for was a boy marvellously endowed for the study of mathematics. At the time of our first meeting at school, I was unable to solve even the simplest algebraical problem. But we had been together only for half a month, when we exchanged parts. It was I who was the mathematical genius now, whereas he became hopelessly dull and stuttered through his recitations only with a struggle that brought the tears to his eyes. Then I discarded him. Heartless, you say? I have come to know better. Have you ever tasted a bottle of wine that had been uncorked for a long time? If you have, you have probably found it flat—the essence was gone, evaporated. Thus it is when we care for people. Probably—no, assuredly—there is some principle prisoned in their souls, or in the windings of their brains, which, when escaped, leaves them insipid, unprofitable and devoid of interest to us. Sometimes this essence—not necessarily the finest element in a man's or a woman's nature, but soul-stuff that we lack— disappears. In fact, it invariably disappears. It may be that it has been transformed in the processes of their growth; it may also be that it has utterly vanished by some inadvertence, or that we ourselves have absorbed it."

"Then we throw them away?" Ethel asked, pale, but dry-eyed. A shudder passed through her body and she clinched her glass nervously. At that moment Reginald resembled a veritable Prince of Darkness, sinister and beautiful, painted by the hand of a modern master. Then, for a

space, he again became the man of the world. Smiling and self-possessed, he filled the glasses, took a long sip of the wine and resumed his narrative.

"That boy was followed by others. I absorbed many useless things and some that were evil. I realised that I must direct my absorptive propensities. This I did. I selected, selected well. And all the time the terrible power of which I was only half conscious grew within me."

"It is indeed a terrible power," she cried; "all the more terrible for its subtlety. Had I not myself been its victim, I should not now find it possible to believe in it."

"The invisible hand that smites in the dark is certainly more fearful than a visible foe. It is also more merciful. Think how much you would have suffered had you been conscious of your loss."

"Still it seems even now to me that it cannot have been an utter, irreparable loss. There is no action without reaction. Even I—even we—must have received from you some compensation for what you have taken away."

"In the ordinary processes of life the law of action and reaction is indeed potent. But no law is without exception. Think of radium, for instance, with its constant and seemingly inexhaustible outflow of energy. It is a difficult thing to imagine, but our scientific men have accepted it as a fact. Why should we find it more difficult to conceive of a tremendous and infinite absorptive element? I feel sure that it must somewhere exist. But every phenomenon in the physical world finds its counterpart in the psychical universe. There are radium-souls that radiate without loss of energy, but also without increase. And there are souls, the reverse of radium, with unlimited absorptive capacities."

"Vampire-souls," she observed, with a shudder, and her face blanched.

"No," he said, "don't say that." And then he suddenly seemed to grow in stature. His face was ablaze, like the face of a god.

"In every age," he replied, with solemnity, "there are giants who attain to a greatness which by natural growth no men could ever have reached. But in their youth a vision came to them, which they set out to seek. They take the stones of fancy to build them a palace in the kingdom of truth, projecting into reality dreams, monstrous and impossible. Often they fail and, tumbling from their airy heights, end a quixotic career. Some succeed. They are the chosen. Carpenter's sons they are, who have laid down the Law of a World for milleniums to come; or simple Corsicans, before whose eagle eye have quaked the kingdoms of the earth. But to accomplish their mission they need a will of iron and the wit of a hundred men. And from the iron they take the strength, and from a hundred men's brains they absorb their wisdom. Divine missionaries, they appear in all departments of life. In their hand is gathered to-day the gold of the world. Mighty potentates of peace and war, they unlock new seas and from distant continents lift the bars. Single-handed, they accomplish what nations dared not hope; with Titan strides they scale the stars and succeed where millions fail. In art they live, the makers of new periods, the dreamers of new styles. They make themselves the vocal sun-glasses of God. Homer and Shakespeare, Hugo and Balzac—they concentrate the dispersed rays of a thousand lesser luminaries in one singing flame that, like a giant torch, lights up humanity's path."

She gazed at him, open-mouthed. The light had gone from his visage. He paused, exhausted, but even then he looked the incarnation of a force no less terrible, no less grand. She grasped the immensity of his conception, but her woman's soul rebelled at the horrible injustice to those whose light is extinguished, as hers had been, to feed an alien flame. And then, for a moment, she saw' the pale face of Ernest staring at her out of the wine.

"Cruel," she sobbed, "how cruel!"

"'What matter?" he asked. "Their strength is taken from them, but the spirit of humanity, as embodied in us, triumphantly marches on."

Chapter 21

Reginald's revelations were followed by a long silence, interrupted only by the officiousness of the waiter. The spell once broken, they exchanged a number of more or less irrelevant observations. Ethel's mind returned, again and again, to the word he had not spoken. He had said nothing of the immediate bearing of his monstrous power upon her own life and that of Ernest Fielding.

At last, somewhat timidly, she approached the subject. "You said you loved me," she remarked.

"I did."

"But why, then—"

"I could not help it."

"Did you ever make the slightest attempt?"

"In the horrible night hours I struggled against it. I even implored you to leave me."

"Ah, but I loved you!"

"You would not be warned, you would not listen. You stayed with me, and slowly, surely, the creative urge went out of your life."

"But what on earth could you find in my poor art to attract you? What were my pictures to you?"

"I needed them, I needed you. It was a certain something, a rich colour effect, perhaps. And then, under your very eyes, the colour that vanished from your canvases reappeared in my prose. My style became more luxurious than it had been, while you tortured your soul in the vain attempt of calling back to your brush what was irretrievably lost."

"Why did you not tell me?"

"You would have laughed in my face, and I could not have endured your laugh. Besides, I always hoped, until it was too late, that I might yet check the mysterious power within me. Soon, however, I became aware that it was beyond my control. The unknown god, whose instrument I am, had wisely made it stronger than me."

"But why," retorted Ethel, "was it necessary to discard me, like a cast-off garment, like a wanton who has lost the power to please?"

Her frame shook with the remembered emotion of that moment, when years ago he had politely told her that she was nothing to him.

"The law of being," Reginald replied, almost sadly, "the law of my being. I should have pitied you, but the eternal reproach of your suffering only provoked my anger. I cared less for you every day, and when I had absorbed all of you that my growth required, you were to me as one dead, as a stranger you were. There was between us no further community of interest; henceforth, I knew, our lives must move in totally different spheres. You remember that day when we said good-bye?"

"You mean that day when I lay before you on my knees," she corrected him.

"That day I buried my last dream of personal happiness. I would have gladly raised you from the floor, but love was utterly gone. If I am tenderer to-day than I am wont to be, it is because you mean so much to me as the symbol of my renunciation. When I realised that I could not even save the thing I loved from myself, I became hardened and cruel to others. Not that I know no

kindly feeling, but no qualms of conscience lay their prostrate forms across my path. There is nothing in life for me but my mission."

His face was bathed in ecstasy. The pupils were luminous, large and threatening. He had the look of a madman or a prophet.

After a while Ethel remarked: "But you have grown into one of the master-figures of the age. Why not be content with that? Is there no limit to your ambition?"

Reginald smiled: "Ambition! Shakespeare stopped when he had reached his full growth, when he had exhausted the capacity of his contemporaries. I am not yet ready to lay down my pen and rest."

"And will you always continue in this criminal course, a murderer of other lives?" He looked her calmly in the face. "I do not know."

"Are you the slave of your unknown god?"

"We are all slaves, wire-pulled marionettes: You, Ernest, I. There is no freedom on the face of the earth nor above. The tiger that tears a lamb is not free, I am not free, you are not free. All that happens must happen; no word that is said is said in, vain, in vain is raised no hand."

"Then," Ethel retorted, eagerly, "if I attempted to wrest your victim from you, I should also be the tool of your god?"'

"Assuredly. But I am his chosen."

"Can you—can you not set him free?"

"I need him—a little longer. Then he is yours."

"But can you not, if I beg you again on my knees, at least loosen his chains before he is utterly ruined?"

"It is beyond my power. If I could not rescue you, whom I loved, what in heaven or on earth can save him from his fate? Besides, he will not be utterly ruined. It is only a part of him that I absorb. In his soul are chords that I have not touched. They may vibrate one day, when he has gathered new strength. You, too, would have spared yourself much pain had you striven to attain success in different fields—not where I had garnered the harvest of a lifetime. It is only a portion of his talent that I take from him. The rest I cannot harm. Why should he bury that remainder?"

His eyes strayed through the window to the firmament, as if to say that words could no more bend his indomitable will than alter the changeless course of the stars.

Ethel had half-forgotten the wrong she herself had suffered at his hands. He could not be measured by ordinary standards, this dazzling madman, whose diseased will-power had assumed such uncanny proportions. But here a young life was at stake. In her mind's eye she saw Reginald crush between his relentless hands the delicate soul of Ernest Fielding, as a magnificent carnivorous flower might close its glorious petals upon a fly.

Love, all conquering love, welled up in her. She would fight for Ernest as a tiger cat fights for its young. She would place herself in the way of the awful force that had shattered her own aspirations, and save, at any cost, the brilliant boy who did not love her.

Chapter 22

The last rays of the late afternoon sun fell slanting through Ernest's window. He was lying on his couch, in a leaden, death-like slumber that, for the moment at least, was not even perturbed by the presence of Reginald Clarke.

The latter was standing at the boy's bedside, calm, unmoved as ever. The excitement of his conversation with Ethel had left no trace on the chiselled contour of his forehead. Smilingly

fastening an orchid of an indefinable purple tint in his evening coat, radiant, buoyant with life, he looked down upon the sleeper. Then he passed his hand over Ernest's forehead, as if to wipe off beads of sweat. At the touch of his hand the boy stirred uneasily. When it was not withdrawn his countenance twitched in pain. He moaned as men moan under the influence of some anæsthetic, without possessing the power to break through the narrow partition that separates them from death on the one side and from consciousness on the other. At last a sigh struggled to his seemingly paralysed lips, then another. Finally the babbling became articulate.

"For God's sake," he cried, in his sleep, "take that hand away!" And all at once the benignant smile on Reginald's features was changed to a look of savage fierceness. He no longer resembled the man of culture, but a disappointed, snarling beast of prey. He took his hand from Ernest's forehead and retired cautiously through the half-open door.

Hardly had he disappeared when Ernest awoke. For a moment he looked around, like a hunted animal, then sighed with relief and buried his head in his hand. At that moment a knock at the door was heard, and Reginald re-entered, calm as before.

"I declare," he exclaimed, "you have certainly been sleeping the sleep of the just."

"It isn't laziness," Ernest replied, looking up rather pleased at the interruption. "But I've a splitting headache."

"Perhaps those naps are not good for your health."

"Probably. But of late I have frequently found it necessary to exact from the day-hours the sleep which the night refuses me. I suppose it is all due to indigestion, as you have suggested. The stomach is the source of all evil."

"It is also the source of all good. The Greeks made it the seat of the soul. I have always claimed that the most important item in a great poet's biography is an exact reproduction of his menu."

"True, a man who eats a heavy beefsteak for breakfast in the morning is incapable of writing a sonnet in the afternoon."

"Yes," Reginald added, "we are what we eat and what our forefathers have eaten before us. I ascribe the staleness of American poetry to the griddle-cakes of our Puritan ancestors. I am sorry we cannot go deeper into the subject at present. But I have an invitation to dinner where I shall study, experimentally, the influence of French sauces on my versification."

"Good-bye."

"*Au revoir.*" And, with a wave of the hand, Reginald left the room. When the door had closed behind him, Ernest's thoughts took a more serious turn. The tone of light bantering in which the preceding conversation had taken place had been assumed on his part. For the last few weeks evil dreams had tortured his sleep and cast their shadow upon his waking hours. They had ever increased in reality, in intensity and in hideousness. Even now he could see the long, tapering fingers that every night were groping in the windings of his brain. It was a well-formed, manicured hand that seemed to reach under his skull, carefully feeling its way through the myriad convolutions where thought resides.

And, oh, the agony of it all! A human mind is not a thing of stone, but alive, horribly alive to pain. What was it those fingers sought, what mysterious treasures, what jewels hidden in the under-layer of his consciousness? His brain was like a human gold-mine, quaking under the blow of the pick and the tread of the miner. The miner! Ah, the miner! Ceaselessly, thoroughly, relentlessly, he opened vein after vein and wrested untold riches from the quivering ground; but each vein was a live vein and each nugget of gold a thought!

No wonder the boy was a nervous wreck. Whenever a tremulous nascent idea was formulating itself, the dream-hand clutched it and took it away, brutally severing the fine threads that bind thought to thought. And when the morning came, how his head ached! It was not an acute pain, but dull, heavy, incessant.

These sensations, Ernest frequently told himself, were morbid fancies. But then, the monomaniac who imagines that his arms have been mangled or cut from his body, might as well be without arms. Mind can annihilate obstacles. It can also create them. Psychology was no unfamiliar ground to Ernest, and it was not difficult for him to seek in some casual suggestion an explanation for his delusion, the fixed notion that haunted him day and night. But he also realized that to explain a phenomenon is not to explain it away. The man who analyses his emotions cannot wholly escape them, and the shadow of fear—primal, inexplicable fear—may darken at moments of weakness the life of the subtlest psychologist and the clearest thinker.

He had never spoken to Reginald of his terrible nightmares. Coming on the heel of the fancy that he, Ernest, had written "The Princess With the Yellow Veil," a fancy that, by the way, had again possessed him of late, this new delusion would certainly arouse suspicion as to his sanity in Reginald's mind. He would probably send him to a sanitarium; he certainly would not keep him in the house. Beneficence itself in all other things, his host was not to be trifled with in any matter that interfered with his work. He would act swiftly and without mercy.

For the first time in many days Ernest thought of Abel Felton. Poor boy! What had become of him after he had been turned from the house? He would not wait for any one to tell him to pack his bundle. But then, that was impossible; Reginald was fond of him.

Suddenly Ernest's meditations were interrupted by a noise at the outer door. A key was turned in the lock. It must be he—but why so soon? What could have brought him back at this hour? He opened the door and went out into the hall to see what had happened. The figure that he beheld was certainly not the person expected, but a woman, from whose shoulders a theatre-cloak fell in graceful folds,—probably a visitor for Reginald. Ernest was about to withdraw discreetly, when the electric light that was burning in the hallway fell upon her face and illumined it.

Then indeed surprise overcame him. "Ethel," he cried, "is it you?"

Chapter 23

Ernest conducted Ethel Brandenbourg to his room and helped her to remove her cloak.

While he was placing the garment upon the back of a chair, she slipped a little key into her hand-bag. He looked at her with a question in his eyes.

"Yes," she replied, "I kept the key; but I had not dreamed that I would ever again cross this threshold."

Meanwhile it had grown quite dark. The reflection of the street lanterns without dimly lit the room, and through the twilight fantastic shadows seemed to dance.

The perfume of her hair pervaded the room and filled the boy's heart with romance. Tenderness long suppressed called with a thousand voices. The hour, the strangeness and unexpectedness of her visit, perhaps even a boy's pardonable vanity, roused passion from its slumbers and once again wrought in Ernest's soul the miracle of love. His arm encircled her neck and his lips stammered blind, sweet, crazy and caressing things.

"Turn on the light," she pleaded. "You were not always so cruel."

"No matter, I have not come to speak of love."

"Why, then, have you come?"

Ernest felt a little awkward, disappointed, as he uttered these words. What could have induced her to come to his rooms? He loosened his hold on her and did as she asked.

How pale she looked in the light, how beautiful! Surely, she had sorrowed for him; but why had she not answered his letter? Yes, why?

"Your letter?" She smiled a little sadly. "Surely you did not expect me to answer that?"

"Why not?" He had again approached her and his lips were close to hers. "Why not? I have yearned for you. I love you."

His breath intoxicated her; it was like a subtle perfume. Still she did not yield. "You love me now—you did not love me then. The music of your words was cold—machine- made, strained and superficial. I shall not answer, I told myself: in his heart he has forgotten you. I did not then realise that a dangerous force had possessed your life and crushed in your mind every image but its own.

"I don't understand."

"Do you think I would have come here if it were a light matter? No, I tell you, it is a matter of life and death to you, at least as an artist."

"What do you mean by that?"

"Have you done a stroke of work since I last saw you?"

"Yes, let me see, surely, magazine articles and a poem."

"That is not what I want to know. Have you accomplished anything big? Have you grown since this summer? How about your novel?"

"I—I have almost finished it in my mind, but I have found no chance to begin with the actual writing. I was sick of late, very sick."

No doubt of it! His face was pinched and pale, and the lines about the mouth were curiously contorted, like those of a man suffering from a painful internal disease.

"Tell me," she ventured, "do you ever miss anything?"

"Do you mean—are there thieves?"

"Thieves! Against thieves one can protect oneself." He stared at her wildly, half-frightened, in anticipation of some dreadful revelation. His dream! His dream! That hand! Could it be more than a dream? God! His lips quivered.

Ethel observed his agitation and continued more quietly, but with the same insistence: "Have you ever had ideas, plans that you began without having strength to complete them? Have you had glimpses of vocal visions that seemed to vanish no sooner than seen? Did it ever seem to you as if some mysterious and superior will brutally interfered with the workings of your brain?"

Did it seem so to him! He himself could not have stated more plainly the experience of the last few months. Each word fell from her lips like the blow of a hammer. Shivering, he put his arm around her, seeking solace, not love. This time she did not repulse him and, trustingly, as a child confides to his mother, he depicted to her the suffering that harrowed his life and made it a hell.

As she listened, indignation clouded her forehead, while rising tears of anger and of love weighed down her lashes. She could bear the pitiful sight no longer.

"Child," she cried, "do you know who your tormentor is?" And like a flash the truth passed from her to him. A sudden intimation told him what her words had still concealed.

"Don't! For Christ's sake, do not pronounce his name!" he sobbed. "Do not breathe it. I could not endure it. I should go mad."

Chapter 24

Very quietly, with difficulty restraining her own emotion so as not to excite him further, Ethel had related to Ernest the story of her remarkable interview with Reginald Clarke. In the long silence that ensued, the wings of his soul brushed against hers for the first time, and Love by a thousand tender chains of common suffering welded their beings into one.

Caressingly the ivory of her fingers passed through the gold of his hair and over his brow, as if to banish the demon-eyes that stared at him across the hideous spaces of the past. In a rush a thousand incidents came back to him, mute witnesses of a damning truth. His play, the dreams that tormented him, his own inability to concentrate his mind upon his novel which hitherto he had ascribed to nervous disease—all, piling fact on fact, became one monstrous monument of Reginald Clarke's crime. At last Ernest understood the parting words of Abel Felton and the look in Ethel's eye on the night when he had first linked his fate with the other man's. Walkham's experience, too, and Reginald's remarks on the busts of Shakespeare and Balzac unmistakably pointed toward the new and horrible spectre that Ethel's revelation had raised in place of his host.

An then, again, the other Reginald appeared, crowned with the lyric wreath. From his lips golden cadences fell, sweeter than the smell of many flowers or the sound of a silver bell. He was once more the divine master, whose godlike features bore no trace of malice and who had raised him to a place very near his heart.

"No," he cried, "it is impossible. It's all a dream, a horrible nightmare."

"But he has himself confessed it," she interjected.

"Perhaps he has spoken in symbols. We all absorb to some extent other men's ideas, without robbing them and wrecking their thought-life. Reginald may be unscrupulous in the use of his power of impressing upon others the stamp of his master-mind. So was Shakespeare. No, no, no! You are mistaken; we were both deluded for the moment by his picturesque account of a common, not even a discreditable, fact. He may himself have played with the idea, but surely he cannot have been serious.

"And your own experience, and Abel Felton's and mine—can they, too, be dismissed with a shrug of the shoulder?"

"But, come to think of it, the whole theory seems absurd. It is unscientific. It is not even a case of mesmerism. If he had said that he hypnotised his victims, the matter would assume a totally different aspect. I admit that something is wrong somewhere, and that the home of Reginald Clarke is no healthful abode for me. But you must also remember that probably we are both unstrung to the point of hysteria."

But to Ethel his words carried no conviction.

"You are still under his spell," she cried, anxiously. A little shaken in his confidence, Ernest resumed: "Reginald is utterly incapable of such an action, even granting that he possessed the terrible power of which you speak. A man of his splendid resources, a literary Midas at whose very touch every word turns into gold, is under no necessity to prey on the thoughts of others. Circumstances, I admit, are suspicious. But in the light of common day this fanciful theory shrivels into nothing. Any court of law would reject our evidence as madness. It is too utterly fantastic, utterly alien to any human experience."

"Is it though?" Ethel replied with peculiar intonation. "Why, what do you mean?"

"Surely," she answered, "you must know that in the legends of every nation we read of men and women who were called vampires. They are beings, not always wholly evil, whom every night some mysterious impulse leads to steal into unguarded bedchambers, to suck the blood of the sleepers and then, having waxed strong on the life of their victims, cautiously to retreat. Thence comes it that their lips are very red. It is even said that they can find no rest in the grave, but return to their former haunts long after they are believed to be dead. Those whom they visit, however, pine away for no apparent reason. The physicians shake their wise heads and speak of consumption. But sometimes, ancient chronicles assure us, the people's suspicions were aroused, and under the leadership of a good priest they went in solemn procession to the graves of the persons suspected. And on opening the tombs it was found that their coffins had rotted away and the flowers in their hair were black. But their bodies were white and whole; through no empty sockets crept the vermin, and their sucking lips were still moist with a little blood."

Ernest was carried away in spite of himself by her account, which vividly resembled his own experience. Still he would not give in.

"All this is impressive. I admit it is very impressive. But you yourself speak of such stories as legends. They are unfounded upon any tangible fact, and you cannot expect a man schooled in modern sciences to admit, as having any possible bearing upon his life, the crude belief of the Middle Ages!"

"Why not?" she responded. "Our scientists have proved true the wildest theories of medieval scholars. The transmutation of metals seems to-day no longer an idle speculation, and radium has transformed into potential reality the dream of perpetual motion. The fundamental notions of mathematics are being undermined. One school of philosophers claims that the number of angles in a triangle is equal to more than two right angles; another propounds that it is less. Even great scientists who have studied the soul of nature are turning to spiritism. The world is overcoming the shallow scepticism of the nineteenth century. Life has become once more wonderful and very mysterious. But it also seems that, with the miracles of the old days, their terrors, their nightmares and their monsters have come back in a modern guise."

Ernest became even more thoughtful. "Yes," he observed, "there is something in what you say." Then, pacing the room nervously, he exclaimed: "And still I find it impossible to believe your explanation. Reginald a vampire! It seems so ludicrous. If you had told me that such creatures exist somewhere, far away, I might have discussed the matter; but in this great city, in the shadow of the Flatiron Building—no!"

She replied with warmth: "Yet they exist— always have existed. Not only in the Middle Ages, but at all times and in all regions. There is no nation but has some record of them, in one form or another. And don't you think if we find a thought, no matter how absurd it may seem to us, that has ever occupied the minds of men—if we find, I say, such a perennially recurrent thought, are we not justified in assuming that it must have some basis in the actual experience of mankind?"

Ernest's brow became very clouded, and infinite numbers of hidden premature wrinkles began to show. How wan he looked and how frail! He was as one lost in a labyrinth in which he saw no light, convinced against his will, or rather, against his scientific conviction, that she was not wholly mistaken.

"Still," he observed triumphantly, "your vampires suck blood; but Reginald, if vampire he be, preys upon the soul. How can a man suck from another man's brain a thing as intangible, as quintessential as thought?"

"Ah," she replied, "you forget, thought is more real than blood!"

Chapter 25

Only three hours had passed since Ethel had startled Ernest from his sombre reveries, but within this brief space their love had matured as if each hour had been a year. The pallor had vanished from his cheeks and the restiveness from his eyes. The intoxication of her presence had rekindled the light of his countenance and given him strength to combat the mighty forces embodied in Reginald Clarke. The child in him had made room for the man. He would not hear of surrendering without a struggle, and Ethel felt sure she might leave his fate in his own hand. Love had lent him a coat of mail. He was warned, and would not succumb. Still she made one more attempt to persuade him to leave the house at once with her.

"I must go now," she said. "Will you not come with me, after all? I am so afraid to think of you still here."

"No, dear," he replied. "I shall not desert my post. I must solve the riddle of this man's life; and if, indeed, he is the thing he seems to be, I shall attempt to wrest from him what he has stolen from me. I speak of my unwritten novel."

"Do not attempt to oppose him openly. You cannot resist him."

"Be assured that I shall be on my guard. I have in the last few hours lived through so much that makes life worth living, that I would not wantonly expose myself to any danger. Still, I cannot go without certainty—cannot, if there is some truth in our fears, leave the best of me behind."

"What are you planning to do?"

"My play—I am sure now that it is mine— I cannot take from him; that is irretrievably lost. He has read it to his circle and prepared for its publication. And, no matter how firmly convinced you or I may be of his strange power, no one would believe our testimony. They would pronounce us mad. Perhaps we are mad!"

"No; we are not mad; but it is mad for you to stay here," she asserted.

"I shall not stay here one minute longer than is absolutely essential. Within a week I shall have conclusive proof of his guilt or innocence."

"How will you go about it?"

"His writing table—"

"Yes, perhaps I can discover some note, some indication, some proof "

"It's a dangerous game."

"I have everything to gain."

"I wish I could stay here with you," she said. "Have you no friend, no one whom you could trust in this delicate matter?"

"Why, yes—Jack."

A shadow passed over her face. "Do you know," she said, "I have a feeling that you care more for him than for me "Nonsense," he said, "he is my friend, you, you—immeasurably more."

"Are you still as intimate with him as when I first met you?"

"Not quite; of late a troubling something, like a thin veil, seems to have passed between us. But he will come when I call him. He will not fail me in my hour of need."

"When can he be here?"

"In two or three days."

"Meanwhile be very careful. Above all, lock your door at night."

"I will not only lock, but barricade it. I shall try with all my power to elucidate this mystery without, however, exposing myself to needless risks."

"I will go, then. Kiss me good-bye."

"May I not take you to the car?"

"You had better not."

At the door she turned back once more. "Write me every day, or call me up on the telephone." He straightened himself, as if to convince her of his strength. Yet when at last the door had closed behind her, his courage forsook him for a moment. And, if he had not been ashamed to appear a weakling before the woman he loved, who knows if any power on earth could have kept him in that house where from every corner a secret seemed to lurk!

There was a misgiving, too, in the woman's heart as she left the boy behind,—a prey to the occult power that, seeking expression in multiple activities, has made and unmade emperors, prophets and poets.

As she stepped into a street car she saw from afar, as in a vision, the face of Reginald Clarke. It seemed very white and hungry. There was no human kindness in it—only a threat and a sneer.

Chapter 26

For over an hour Ernest paced up and down his room, wildly excited by Ethel's revelations. It required an immense amount of self-control for him to pen the following lines to Jack: "I need you. Come."

After he had entrusted the letter to the hall-boy, a reaction set in and he was able to consider the matter, if not with equanimity, at least with a degree of calmness. The strangest thing to him was that he could not bring himself to hate Reginald, of whose evil influence upon his life he was now firmly convinced. Here was another shattered idol; but one—like the fragment of a great god-face in the desert—intensely fascinating, even in its ruin. Then yielding to a natural impulse, Ernest looked over his photographs and at once laid hold upon the austere image of his master and friend. No—it was preposterous; there was no evil in this man. There was no trace of malice in this face, the face of a prophet or an inspired madman, a poet. And yet, as he scrutinised the picture closely a curious transformation seemed to take place in the features; a sly little line appeared insinuatingly about Reginald's well-formed mouth, and the serene calm of his Jupiter-head seemed to turn into the sneak smile of a thief. Nevertheless, Ernest was not afraid. His anxieties had at last assumed definite shape; it was possible now to be on his guard. It is only invisible, incomprehensible fear, crouching upon us from the night, that drives sensitive natures to the verge of madness and transforms stern warriors into cowards.

Ernest realised the necessity of postponing the proposed investigation of Reginald's papers until the morning, as it was now near eleven, and he expected to hear at any moment the sound of his feet at the door. Before retiring he took a number of precautions. Carefully he locked the door to his bedroom and placed a chair in front of it. To make doubly sure, he fastened the handle to an exquisite Chinese vase, a gift of Reginald's, that at the least attempt to force an entrance from without would come down with a crash.

Then, although sleep seemed out of the question, he went to bed. He had hardly touched the pillow when a leaden weight seemed to fall upon his eyes. The day's commotion had been too much for his delicate frame. By force of habit he pulled the cover over his ear and fell asleep.

All night he slept heavily, and the morning was far advanced when a knock at the door that, at first, seemed to come across an immeasurable distance, brought him back to himself. It was Reginald's manservant announcing that breakfast was waiting.

Ernest got up and rubbed his eyes. The barricade at the door at once brought back to his mind with startling clearness the events of the previous evening.

Everything was as he had left it. Evidently no one had attempted to enter the room while he slept. He could not help smiling at the arrangement which reminded him of his childhood, when he had sought by similar means security from burglars and bogeys. And in the broad daylight Ethel's tales of vampires seemed once more impossible and absurd. Still, he had abundant evidence of Reginald's strange influence, and was determined to know the truth before nightfall. Her words, that thought is more real than blood, kept ringing in his ears. If such was the case, he would find evidence of Reginald's intellectual burglaries, and possibly be able to regain a part of his lost self that had been snatched from him by the relentless dream-hand.

But under no circumstances could he face Reginald in his present state of mind. He was convinced that if in the fleeting vision of a moment the other man's true nature should reveal itself to him, he would be so terribly afraid as to shriek like a maniac. So he dressed particularly slowly in the hope of avoiding an encounter with his host. But fate thwarted this hope. Reginald, too, lingered that morning unusually long over his coffee. He was just taking his last sip when Ernest entered the room. His behaviour was of an almost bourgeois kindness. Benevolence fairly beamed from his face. But to the boy's eyes it had assumed a new and sinister expression.

"You are late this morning, Ernest," he remarked in his mildest manner. "Have you been about town, or writing poetry? Both occupations are equally unhealthy." As he said this he watched the young man with the inscrutable smile that at moments was wont to curl upon his lips. Ernest had once likened it to the smile of Mona Lisa, but now he detected in it the suavity of the hypocrite and the leer of the criminal.

He could not endure it; he could not look upon that face any longer. His feet almost gave way under him, cold sweat gathered on his brow, and he sank on a chair trembling and studiously avoiding the other man's gaze.

At last Reginald rose to go. It seemed impossible to accuse this splendid impersonation of vigorous manhood of cunning and underhand methods, of plagiarisms and of theft. As he stood there he resembled more than anything a beautiful tiger-cat, a wonderful thing of strength and will-power, indomitable and insatiate. Yet who could tell whether this strength was not, after all, parasitic. If Ethel's suspicions were justified, then, indeed, more had been taken from him than he could ever realise. For in that case it was his lifeblood that circled in those veins and the fire of his intellect that set those lips aflame!

Chapter 27

Reginald Clarke had hardly left the room when Ernest hastily rose from his seat. While it was likely that he would remain in undisturbed possession of the apartment the whole morning, the stake at hand was too great to permit of delay.

Palpitating and a little uncertain, he entered the studio where, scarcely a year ago, Reginald Clarke had bidden him welcome. Nothing had changed there since then; only in Ernest's mind the room had assumed an aspect of evil. The Antinous was there and the Faun and the Christ- head. But their juxtaposition to-day partook of the nature of the blasphemous. The statues of Shakespeare and Balzac seemed to frown from their pedestals as his fingers were running through Reginald's papers. He brushed against a semblance of Napoleon that was standing on the writing-table, so that it toppled over and made a noise that weirdly re-echoed in the silence of the room. At that moment a curious family resemblance between Shakespeare, Balzac, Napoleon—and Reginald, forcibly impressed itself upon his mind. It was the indisputable something that marks those who are chosen to give ultimate expression to some gigantic world- purpose. In Balzac's face it was diffused with kindliness, in that of Napoleon sheer brutality predominated. The image of one who was said to be the richest man of the world also rose before his eyes. Perhaps it was only the play of his fevered imagination, but he could have sworn that this man's features, too, bore the mark of those unoriginal, great absorptive minds who, for better or for worse, are born to rob and rule. They seemed to him monsters that know neither justice nor pity, only the law of their being, the law of growth.

Common weapons would not avail against such forces. Being one, they were stronger than armies; nor could they be overcome in single combat. Stealth, trickery, the outfit of the knave, were legitimate weapons in such a fight. In this case the end justified the means, even if the latter included burglary.

After a brief and fruitless search of the desk, he attempted to force open a secret drawer, the presence of which he had one day accidentally discovered. He tried a number of keys to no account, and was thinking of giving up his researches for the day until he had procured a skeleton key, when at last the lock gave way.

The drawer disclosed a large file of manuscript. Ernest paused for a moment to draw breath. The paper rustled under his nervous fingers. And there—at last—his eyes lit upon a bulky bundle that bore this legend: "Leontina, A Novel."

It was true, then—all, his dream, Reginald's confession. And the house that had opened its doors so kindly to him was the house of a Vampire!

Finally curiosity overcame his burning indignation. He attempted to read. The letters seemed to dance before his eyes—his hands trembled.

At last he succeeded. The words that had first rolled over like drunken soldiers now marched before his vision in orderly sequence. He was delighted, then stunned. This was indeed authentic literature, there could be no doubt about it. And it was his. He was still a poet, a great poet. He drew a deep breath. Sudden joy trembled in his heart. This story set down by a foreign hand had grown chapter by chapter in his brain.

There were some slight changes—slight deviations from the original plan. A defter hand than his had retouched it here and there, but for all that it remained his very own. It did not belong to that thief. The blood welled to his cheek as he uttered this word that, applied to Reginald, seemed almost sacrilegious.

He had nearly reached the last chapter when he heard steps in the hallway. Hurriedly he restored the manuscript to its place, closed the drawer and left the room on tiptoe.

It was Reginald. But he did not come alone. Someone was speaking to him. The voice seemed familiar. Ernest could not make out what it said. He listened intently and—was it possible? Jack? Surely he could not yet have come in response to his note! What mysterious power, what dim presentiment of his friend's plight had led him hither? But why did he linger so long in Reginald's room, instead of hastening to greet him? Cautiously he drew nearer. This time he caught Jack's words:

"It would be very convenient and pleasant. Still, some way, I feel that it is not right for me, of all men, to take his place here."

"That need not concern you," Reginald deliberately replied; "the dear boy expressed the desire to leave me within a fortnight. I think he will go to some private sanitarium. His nerves are frightfully overstrained."

"This seems hardly surprising after the terrible attack he had when you read your play."

"That idea has since then developed into a monomania."

"I am awfully sorry for him. I cared for him much, perhaps too much. But I always feared that he would come to such an end. Of late his letters have been strangely unbalanced."

"You will find him very much changed. In fact, he is no longer the same."

"No," said Jack, "he is no longer the friend I loved."

Ernest clutched for the wall. His face was contorted with intense agony. Each word was like a nail driven into his flesh. Crucified upon the cross of his own affection by the hand he loved, all white and trembling he stood there. Tears rushed to his eyes, but he could not weep. Dry-eyed he reached his room and threw himself upon his bed. Thus he lay—uncomforted and alone.

Chapter 28

Terrible as was his loneliness, a meeting with Jack would have been more terrible. And, after all, it was true, a gulf had opened between them.

Ethel alone could bring solace to his soul. There was a great void in his heart which only she could fill. He hungered for the touch of her hand. He longed for her presence strongly, as a wanton lusts for pleasure and as sad men crave death.

Noiselessly he stole to the door so as not to arouse the attention of the other two men, whose every whisper pierced his heart like a dagger. When he came to Ethel's home, he found that she had gone out for a breath of air. The servant ushered him into the parlor, and there he waited, waited, waited for her.

Greatly calmed by his walk, he turned the details of Clarke's conversation over in his mind, and the conviction grew upon him that the friend of his boyhood was not to blame for his course of action. Reginald probably had encircled Jack's soul with his demoniacal influence and singled him out for another victim. That must never be. It was his turn to save now. He would warn his friend of the danger that threatened him, even if his words should be spoken into the wind. For Reginald, with an ingenuity almost satanic, had already suggested that the delusion of former days had developed into a monomania, and any attempt on his part to warn Jack would only seem to confirm this theory. In that case only one way was left open. He must plead with Reginald himself, confront at all risks that snatcher of souls. To-night he would not fall asleep. He would keep his vigil. And if Reginald should approach his room, if in some way he felt the direful presence, he must speak out, threaten if need be, to save his friend from ruin. He had fully determined upon this course when a cry of joy from Ethel, who had just returned from her walk, interrupted his reverie. But her gladness changed to anxiety when she saw how pale he was. Ernest recounted to her the happenings of the day, from the discovery of his novel in Reginald's desk to the conversation which he had accidentally overheard. He noticed that her features brightened as he drew near the end of his tale.

"Was your novel finished?" she suddenly asked. "I think so."

"Then you are out of danger. He will want nothing else of you. But you should have taken it with you."

"I had only sufficient presence of mind to slip it back into the drawer. To-morrow I shall simply demand it."

"You will do nothing of the kind. It is in his handwriting, and you have no legal proof that it is yours. You must take it away secretly. And he will not dare to reclaim it."

"And Jack?"

She had quite forgotten Jack. Women are invariably selfish for those they love. "You must warn him," she replied.

"He would laugh at me. However, I must speak to Reginald."

"It is of no avail to speak to him. At least, you must not do so before you have obtained the manuscript. It would unnecessarily jeopardise our plans."

"And after?"

"After, perhaps. But you must not expose yourself to any danger."

"No, dear," he said, and kissed her; "what danger is there, provided I keep my wits about me? He steals upon men only in their sleep and in the dark."

"Be careful, nevertheless."

"I shall. In fact, I think he is not at home at this moment. If I go now I may be able to get hold of the manuscript and hide it before he returns."

"I cannot but tremble to think of you in that house."

"You shall have no more reason to tremble in a day or two."

"Shall I see you to-morrow?"

"I don't think so. I must go over my papers and things so as to be ready at any moment to leave the house."

"And then?"

"Then—"

He took her in his arms and looked long and deeply into her eyes. "Yes," she replied—"at least, perhaps."

Then he turned to go, resolute and happy. How strangely he had matured since the summer! Her heart swelled with the consciousness that it was her love that had effected this transformation.

"As I cannot expect you to-morrow, I shall probably go to the opera, but I shall be at home before midnight. Will you call me up then? A word from you will put me at ease for the night, even if it comes over the telephone."

"I will call you up. We moderns have an advantage over the ancients in this respect: the twentieth-century Pyramus can speak to Thisbe even if innumerable walls sever his body from hers."

"A quaint conceit! But let us hope that our love-story will end less tragically," she said, tenderly caressing his hair. "Oh, we shall be happy, you and I," she added, after a while. "The iron finger of fate that lay so heavily on our lives is now withdrawn. Almost withdrawn. Yes, almost. Only almost."

And then a sudden fear overcame her.

"No," she cried, "do not go, do not go! Stay with me; stay here. I feel so frightened. I don't know what comes over me. I am afraid—afraid for you."

"No, dear," he rejoined, "you need not be afraid. In your heart you don't want me to desert a friend, and, besides, leave the best part of my artistic life in Reginald's clutch."

"Why should you expose yourself to God knows what danger for a friend who is ready to betray you?"

"You forget friendship is a gift. If it exacts payment in any form, it is no longer either friendship or a gift. And you yourself have assured me that I have nothing to fear from Reginald. I have nothing to give to him."

She rallied under his words and had regained her self-possession when the door closed behind him. He walked a few blocks very briskly. Then his pace slackened. Her words had unsettled him a little, and when he reached home he did not at once resume his exploration of Reginald's papers. He had hardly lit a cigarette when, at an unusually early hour, he heard Reginald's key in the lock.

Quickly he turned the light out and in the semi-darkness, lit up by an electric lantern below, barricaded the door as on the previous night. Then he went to bed without finding sleep.

Supreme silence reigned over the house. Even the elevator had ceased to run. Ernest's brain was all ear. He heard Reginald walking up and down in the studio. Not the smallest movement escaped his attention. Thus hours passed. When the clock struck twelve, he was still walking up and down, down and up, up and down.

One o'clock.

Still the measured beat of his footfall had not ceased. There was something hypnotic in the regular tread. Nature at last exacted its toll from the boy. He fell asleep.

Hardly had he closed his eyes when again that horrible nightmare— no longer a nightmare—- tormented him. Again he felt the pointed delicate fingers carefully feeling their way along the innumerable tangled threads of nerve-matter that lead to the innermost recesses of self. . .

A subconscious something strove to arouse him, and he felt the fingers softly withdrawn. He could have sworn that he heard the scurrying of feet in the room. Bathed in perspiration he made a leap for the electric light.

But there was no sign of any human presence. The barricade at the door was undisturbed. But fear like a great wind filled the wings of his soul.

Yet there was nothing, nothing to warrant his conviction that Reginald Clarke had been with him only a few moments ago, plying his horrible trade. The large mirror above the fireplace only showed him his own face, white, excited,—the face of a madman.

Chapter 29

The next morning's mail brought a letter from Ethel, a few lines of encouragement and affection. Yes, she was right; it would not do for him to stay under one roof with Reginald any longer. He must only obtain the manuscript and, if possible, surprise him in the attempt to exercise his mysterious and criminal power. Then he would be in the position to dictate terms and to demand Jack's safety as the price of his silence.

Reginald, however, had closeted himself that day in his studio busily writing. Only the clatter of his typewriter announced his presence in the house. There was no chance for conversation or for obtaining the precious manuscript of "Leontina."

Meanwhile Ernest was looking over his papers and preparing everything for a quick departure. Glancing over old letters and notes, he became readily interested and hardly noticed the passage of the hours.

When the night came he only partly undressed and threw himself upon the bed. It was now ten. At twelve he had promised Ethel to speak to her over the telephone. He was determined not to sleep at all that night. At last he would discover whether or not on the previous and other nights Reginald had secretly entered his room.

When one hour had passed without incident, his attention relaxed a little. His eyes were gradually closing when suddenly something seemed to stir at the door. The Chinese vase came rattling to the floor.

At once Ernest sprang up. His face had blanched with terror. It was whiter than the linen in which they wrap the dead. But his soul was resolute.

He touched a buttton and the electric light illuminated the whole chamber. There was no nook for even a shadow to hide. Yet there was no one to be seen. From without the door came no sound. Suddenly something soft touched his foot. He gathered all his will power so as not to break out into a frenzied shriek. 'Then he laughed, not a hearty laugh, to be sure. A tiny nose and a tail gracefully curled were brushing against him. The source of the disturbance was a little Maltese cat, his favourite, that by some chance had remained in his room. After its essay at midnight gymnastics the animal quieted down and lay purring at the foot of his bed.

The presence of a living thing was a certain comfort, and the reservoir of his strength was well nigh exhausted.

He dimly remembered his promise to Ethel, but his lids drooped with sheer weariness. Perhaps an hour passed in this way, when suddenly his blood congealed with dread.

He felt the presence of the hand of Reginald Clarke—unmistakably—groping in his brain as if searching for something that had still escaped him.

He tried to move, to cry out, but his limbs were paralysed. When, by a superhuman effort, he at last succeeded in shaking off the numbness that held him enchained, he awoke just in time to see a figure, that of a man, disappearing in the wall that separated Reginald's apartments from his room . . .

This time it was no delusion of the senses. He heard something like a secret door softly closing behind retreating steps. A sudden fierce anger seized him. He was oblivious of the danger of the terrible power of the older man, oblivious of the love he had once borne him, oblivious of everything save the sense of outraged humanity and outraged right.

The law permits us to shoot a burglar who goes through our pockets at night. Must he tolerate the ravages of this a thousand times more dastardly and dangerous spiritual thief? Was Reginald to enjoy the fruit of other men's labour unpunished? Was he to continue growing into the mightiest literary factor of the century by preying upon his betters? Abel, Walkham, Ethel, he, Jack, were they all to be victims of this insatiable monster?

Was this force resistless as it was relentless?

No, a thousand times, no!

He dashed himself against the wall at the place where the shadow of Reginald Clarke had disappeared. In doing so he touched upon a secret spring. The wall gave way noiselessly. Speechless with rage he crossed the next room and the one adjoining it, and stood in Reginald's studio. The room was brilliantly lighted, and Reginald, still dressed, was seated at his writing- table scribbling notes upon little scraps of paper in his accustomed manner.

At Ernest's approach he looked up without evincing the least sign of terror or surprise. Calmly, almost majestically, he folded his arms over his breast, but there was a menacing glitter in his eyes as he confronted his victim.

Chapter 30

Silently the two men faced each other. Then Ernest hissed:

"Thief!"

Reginald shrugged his shoulders.

"Vampire!"

"So Ethel has infected you with her absurd fancies! Poor boy! I am afraid. . . . I have been wanting to tell you for some time. . . . But I think . . . We have reached the parting of our road!"

"And that you dare to tell me!"

The more he raged, the calmer Reginald seemed to become.

"Really," he said, "I fail to understand. . . . I must ask you to leave my room!"

"You fail to understand? You cad!" Ernest cried. He stepped to the writing-table and opened the secret drawer with a blow. A bundle of manuscripts fell on the floor with a strange rustling noise. Then, seizing his own story, he hurled it upon the table. And behold—the last pages bore corrections in ink that could have been made only a few minutes ago!

Reginald smiled. "Have you come to play havoc with my manuscripts?" he remarked.

"Your manuscripts? Reginald Clarke, you are an impudent impostor! You have written no word that is your own. You are an embezzler of the mind, strutting through life in borrowed and stolen plumes!"

And at once the mask fell from Reginald's face.

"Why stolen?" he coolly said, with a slight touch of irritation. "I absorb. I appropriate. That is the most any artist can say for himself. God creates; man moulds. He gives us the colours; we mix them."

"That is not the question. I charge you with having wilfully and criminally interfered in my life; I charge you with having robbed me of what was mine; I charge you with being utterly vile and rapacious, a hypocrite and a parasite!"

"Foolish boy," Reginald rejoined austerely. "It is through me that the best in you shall survive, even as the obscure Elizabethans live in him of Avon. Shakespeare absorbed what was great in little men—a greatness that otherwise would have perished—and gave it a setting, a life."

"A thief may plead the same. I understand you better. It is your inordinate vanity that prompts you to abuse your monstrous power."

"You err. Self-love has never entered into my actions. I am careless of personal fame. Look at me, boy! As I stand before you I am Homer, I am Shakespeare. . . I am every cosmic manifestation in art. Men have doubted in each incarnation my individual existence. Historians have more to tell of the meanest Athenian scribbler or Elizabethan poetaster than of me. The radiance of my work obscured my very self. I care not. I have a mission. I am a servant of the Lord. I am the vessel that bears the Host!"

He stood up at full length, the personification of grandeur and power. A tremendous force trembled in his very finger tips. He was like a gigantic dynamo, charged with the might of ten thousand magnetic storms that shake the earth in its orbit and lash myriads of planets through infinities of space. . . .

Under ordinary circumstances Ernest or any other man would have quailed before him. But the boy in that epic moment had grown out of his stature. He felt the sword of vengeance in his hands; to him was intrusted the cause of Abel and of Walkham, of Ethel and of Jack. His was the struggle of the individual soul against the same blind and cruel fate that in the past had fashioned the ichthyosaurus and the mastodon.

"By what right," he cried, "do you assume that you are the literary Messiah? Who appointed you? What divine power has made you the steward of my mite and of theirs whom you have robbed?"

"I am a light-bearer. I tread the high hills of mankind. . . I point the way to the future. I light up the abysses of the past. Were not my stature gigantic, how could I hold the torch in all men's sight? The very souls that I tread underfoot realise, as their dying gaze follows me, the possibilities with which the future is big. . . . Eternally secure, I carry the essence of what is cosmic . . . of what is divine. . . . I am Homer . . . Goethe . . . Shakespeare. . . . I am an embodiment of the same force of which Alexander, Cærsar, Confucius and the Christos were also embodiments. . . . None so strong as to resist me."

A sudden madness overcame Ernest at this boast. He must strike now or never. He must rid humanity of this dangerous maniac—this demon of strength. With a power ten times intensified, he raised a heavy chair so as to hurl it at Reginald's head and crush it.

Reginald stood there calmly, a smile upon his lips. . . . Primal cruelties rose from the depth of his nature. . . . Still he smiled, turning his luminous gaze upon the boy . . . and, behold . . . Ernest's hand began to shake . . . the chair fell from his grasp. . . He tried to call for help, but no sound issued from his lips. . . . Utterly paralysed he confronted . . . the Force. . . .

Minutes—eternities passed.

And still those eyes were fixed upon him. But this was no longer Reginald!

It was all brain . . . only brain . . . a tremendous brain-machine . . . infinitely complex . . . infinitely strong. Not more than a mile away Ethel endeavoured to call to him through the night. The telephone rang, once, twice, thrice, insistingly. But Ernest heard it not. Something dragged him . . . dragged the nerves from his body . . . dragged, dragged, dragged. . . . It was an irresistible suction . . . pitiless . . . passionless . . . immense.

Sparks, blue, crimson and violet, seemed to play around the living battery. It reached the finest fibres of his mind. . . . Slowly . . . every trace of mentality disappeared . . . First the will . . . then feeling . . . judgment . . . memory . . . fear even. . . . All that was stored in his brain-cells came forth to be absorbed by that mighty engine. .

The Princess With the Yellow Veil appeared . . . flitted across the room and melted away. She was followed by childhood memories . . . girls' heads, boys' faces . . . He saw his dead mother waving her arms to him. . . . An expression of death-agony distorted the placid features . . . Then, throwing a kiss to him, she, too, disappeared. Picture on picture followed . . . Words of love that he had spoken . . . sins, virtues, magnanimities, meannesses, terrors . . . mathematical formulas even, and snatches of songs. Leontina came and was swallowed up. . . . No, it was Ethel who was trying to speak to him . . . trying to warn. . . . She waved her hands in frantic despair. . . . She was gone. . . . A pale face . . . dark, dishevelled hair . . . Jack. . . . How he had changed! He was in the circle of the vampire's transforming might. "Jack," he cried. Surely Jack had something to explain . . . something to tell him . . . some word that if spoken would bring rest to his soul. He saw the words rise to the boy's lips, but before he had time to utter them his image also had vanished. And Reginald . . . Reginald, too, was gone. . . There was only the mighty brain . . . panting . . . whirling . . . Then there was nothing . . . The annihilation of Ernest Fielding was complete.

Vacantly he stared at the walls, at the room and at his master. The latter was wiping the sweat from his forehead. He breathed deeply . . . The flush of youth spread over his features. . . . His eyes sparkled with a new and dangerous brilliancy. . . . He took the thing that had once been Ernest Fielding by the hand and led it to its room.

Chapter 31

With the first flush of the morning Ethel appeared at the door of the house on Riverside Drive. She had not heard from Ernest, and had been unable to obtain connection with him at the telephone. Anxiety had hastened her steps. She brushed against Jack, who was also directing his steps to the abode of Reginald Clarke.

At the same time something that resembled Ernest Fielding passed from the house of the Vampire. It was a dull and brutish thing, hideously transformed, without a vestige of mind.

"Mr. Fielding," cried Ethel, beside herself with fear as she saw him descending.

"Ernest!" Jack gasped, no less startled at the change in his friend's appearance. Ernest's head followed the source of the sound, but no spark of recognition illumined the deadness of his eyes. Without a present and without a past . . . blindly . . . a gibbering idiot . . . he stumbled down the stairs.

THE END

www.ingramcontent.com/pod-product-compliance
Lightning Source LLC
Chambersburg PA
CBHW070508130626
46555CB00003B/1208